ANTIGONE AND OTHER CLASSICS, CONTEMPORIZED

ANTIGONE AND OTHER CLASSICS, CONTEMPORIZED

◆

Edited by Dr. Marvin D. Hinten

Writers Club Press
San Jose New York Lincoln Shanghai

ANTIGONE AND OTHER CLASSICS, CONTEMPORIZED

Writers Club Press
an imprint of iUniverse.com, Inc.

For information address:
iUniverse.com, Inc.
5220 S 16th, Ste. 200
Lincoln, NE 68512
www.iuniverse.com

ISBN: 0-595-20130-X

Printed in the United States of America

Contents

AN INTRODUCTION:
WHY CONTEMPORARY CLASSICS?

◆

Some of the works in this book were originally written in an older form of English (what scholars call "Early Modern English"); others were originally done in a different language. Regarding the English works, virtually everyone recognizes that our language has changed greatly over the past 400 years. Some words have disappeared entirely; others have changed meaning or connotation. One of the reasons we read past literature is to let older times communicate with us. If the vocabulary is so unfamiliar that we cannot even understand what is happening in a poem or drama, we are halting communication and reducing the value of literary study.

Further, if we use the original words of a Renaissance English writer, we create the erroneous impression that the writers of that period were trying to write in an old-fashioned way. They were not; they wrote for their time. So modernizing the language actually creates, in some ways, a closer "feel" for the writer than presenting it in antique mode.

As for the works here originally done in other languages, translators generally feel compelled to present the works with complete fidelity to their original languages. It is right to do so—for scholars and for students majoring in English. But for students majoring in a different field, studying world literature as part of a liberal arts education, the goal is general familiarity with major literary works, not necessarily a line-by-line rendering. For the purposes of this text, then, sections not germane to a drama's plot have been excised. In the plays of Sophocles, for instance, the odes, paeans, and other extraneous material have been eliminated in this edition.

The works as presented here are designed to meet the purpose that the Roman writer Horace says in *Ars Poetica* that good writing should do: delight and instruct. May you find these renderings of classic works to be both enlightening and entertaining.

—Dr. Marv Hinten

Friends University

KING OEDIPUS

◆

INTRODUCTION TO SOPHOCLES
(c. 495–412 B.C.)

Sophocles, the author of *King Oedipus* and *Antigone*, was born in Athens, Greece around 495 B.C. and died around 412. He was the most famous playwright of ancient times, so highly regarded that Aristotle used his plays (particularly *King Oedipus*) to illustrate points about creating effective drama

Sophocles wrote over 120 plays during his long lifetime. Only seven have survived, so our understanding of his views and skills is naturally somewhat limited. (A modern equivalent would be having only 2-3 Shakespeare plays to study; depending upon which ones survived, we might think of Shakespeare as a writer of only comedies or only tragedies.)

Interestingly, *King Oedipus*, which gives events that occurred before the events in *Antigone*, was actually written about fifteen years after it. Both of these stories were familiar to the ancient Athenians; they enjoyed dramas based on mythology and history which could be used to make points about the gods and about human nature.

KING OEDIPUS
by Sophocles, c. 430 B. C.
(Translated by George Young, contemporized and abridged
by Dr. Marv Hinten)

CHARACTERS
Oedipus, King of Thebes
Jocasta, Queen of Thebes
Creon, Jocasta's brother
Tiresias, a blind prophet
Priest
Messenger
Shepherd
Guard
Senator, part of the chorus (Theban senators)

BACKGROUND: Twenty years ago Oedipus entered the town of
Thebes to discover that they had to pay tribute to a creature called the
Sphinx. Oedipus solved the Sphinx's riddle and thus rescued Thebes.
Since the town's ruler had just died, the people made Oedipus their new
king, and he married the queen, Jocasta, to cement his power (despite
being several years younger than she was.). Twenty years and four kids
later, Oedipus now has to try to save his town again.

SCENE 1

Setting: In front of the royal palace at Thebes. Oedipus enters to speak to the priest, with citizens of Thebes standing around.

Oed.   People of Thebes, why is the whole city filled with incense-smoke, and hymns, and sounds of woe? I didn't think it fit to have a messenger investigate and inform me, so I,

Oedipus, known far and wide, have come here myself. I would be pretty hard-hearted not to care about the cares of my people. (to priest) You, sir, can speak for the people; tell me what the trouble is and whether you think I can help.   5

Prie.   Great Oedipus, governor of our country, you see us gathered around the altars here, some with hardly the strength to come. Other people are gathered in the marketplace, at the shrine of Athena. As you know, the city is being stricken by the gods: the soil is not producing, the herds are not producing, even the women are barren. A plague has come upon the city, weakening our people. We don't see you as a god, but we do recognize you as a man foremost in affairs, who knows how to deal with life. Upon first coming to town you released us from that cruel sorceress, the Sphinx; and you did it without asking our advice or receiving any instruction from us. The insight came to you straight from heaven. You re-established our lives. So to you, Oedipus, we come, begging you to save us again. Please help us, whether you gain your wisdom from heaven, or simply from experience, for I know that men who have lived through much of life and examined it tend to have the best counsel. Please, Sir. We already call you our deliverer; deliver us again! Don't let it be said of your rule that you raised the city only to fall; build us in stability. If you really want to be a ruler, protect your people; towers and ships are nothing without inhabitants.   19

Oed.   Ah, my poor children. I already knew all this, as does everyone in the land. The people are sick, but no one is as sick about all this as I am. For each of you suffers individual pains, but my heart groans for the whole city—and for myself—and for each of you. You don't have to rouse me from sleep, for I have already wandered through a maze of cares and sorrows. The one remedy that I could figure out I have already attempted. Creon, my brother-in-law, I have sent to the oracle at the house of Apollo in Pytho, to ask what I might say or do to rescue the city. I really thought he would be back by now. When he returns, I will certainly do everything the god says to do; I would be a terrible leader if I didn't.

    Prie.   As a matter of fact, I have heard that Creon is almost here.

    Oed.   If only he could bring us good news!

    Prie.   I certainly think he will.   30

    Oed.   Either way, we'll know soon, for here he comes now. (Creon enters.) My good colleague and relative, what news from the god have you brought home?

    Cre.   Favorable. I mean, even though it may sound ominous, if it puts an end to our troubles, that is good news.

    Oed.   What did the oracle say? I am not exactly filled with confidence by what you have said so far.

    Cre.   Do you want to hear the oracle's words with everyone around? I can either say it here or go inside with you.

    Oed.   Say it here! My burdens are more for their sake than my own.

    Cre.   I will declare everything the god told me. Apollo says there is pollution within our city, and we are to drive it away, no longer to protect it.   41

    Oed.   How are we to get rid of it?

    Cre.   By either exile or death—death for death, in fact, because the oracle says it is a blood-loss which has made our city like winter.

    Oed.   Whose death is the oracle talking about?

    Cre.   My lord, we had a king here named Laius, right before you arrived.

Oed.   I've heard his name, though of course I never actually saw the man.

Cre.   He was killed, and we have been told we should have brought his murderer to account.

Oed.   Where could the murderer be by now? How can we find any clues to such an ancient crime?   50

Cre.   The oracle said the pollution is "within our city." If we seek it, we may find it. Perhaps we've never found the murderer because we never looked for him.

Oed.   Where did Laius get killed? Was he in his home, in the city, in another country, or where?

Cre.   He went to make a religious pilgrimage, but nobody really knows what happened after he left.

Oed.   There was no survivor at all who might have seen at least a part of what happened?

Cre.   Everyone was killed along with Laius, except for one person. That man seemed scared out of his wits, and he no longer lives in the city. Of what he saw he only had one thing to say for certain.   60

Oed.   What was that? One thing might lead us to another.

Cre.   He said Laius and the others were killed by robbers.

Oed.   How could a robber have dared to kill the king?

Cre.   Perhaps he hoped for gold.

Oed.   Why didn't you do anything about it? How could you let your king be killed without seeking vengeance?

Cre.   That was the time that the Sphinx took control, and we had greater troubles to attend to.

Oed.   Well, I'll bring this whole thing into the light. It was right for Apollo to insist on revenging a murder victim, and you should have insisted on it too. I shall wreak vengeance for your city and the god together. It's not just for the sake of the city, either, but for my own. After all, the man who murdered the previous king may think he can get

away with murdering me too. In any event, I'll get to the bottom of this
and wipe the slate clean.   72

SCENE 2

Oedipus enters to talk to the senators.

Oed.   I know you have been praying, and your prayers' intent
may be answered. Listen to me.

I of course am a stranger to this episode, and in my investigations I
have not been able to get very far, not really having a key to open up the
mystery. But I have gotten far enough to make this proclamation: If any
of you know who it was that killed Laius, perhaps you are afraid. You
might be afraid because you were aware of the plot or indirectly
involved. If that's the case, I ask you to show me the whole truth. I won't
harm you; I'll simply ask you to move from this city. Or it may be you
know a foreigner who has been involved somehow. Tell me what you
know, and I'll reward you, and be grateful. Now as to the murderer himself—listen to what I say about him. Whoever Laius' murderer is: I
order that no one in this city, or in the outlying regions I control, give
any support to that man. No one greet him, pray for him, or offer a sacrifice for him. Let everyone banish him from your houses, since he is the
pollution that the oracle of Apollo has revealed. And on that guilty
man's head I add this further curse: may he pine away and die, filled
with guilt. If he should even be a member of my own household, and I
willingly allow him to remain, may I suffer all these curses myself. I can't
believe you people never tried to find and punish this man. Even if the
gods hadn't forced you, was it right for you to allow a noble member of
your city to be innocently slain, and a king at that? You should have
searched this whole thing out long ago. But anyway, I am king now. I
have the government which Laius held, and the wife with whom he
slept. So I will fight this fight as though it were my own father killed; I'll

follow every clue. Whoever the murderer is, may the gods give them no harvest, and no children; may they experience worse curses than I have yet named!   20

Sen.   I will reply, my lord. I never murdered the man, nor do I know who did. As to figuring out who has done it at this late date—well, that really should be Apollo's task, since he has asked us to avenge the death.

Oed.   True enough. But men don't have power to make the gods do what they don't want to do.

Sen.   Well, I do have a second thought which may be useful.

Oed.   Tell me your second, and your third, if you have one.

Sen.   Sir, the mortal with most heavenly knowledge is Tiresias the prophet. He may be able to shine some truth into this.

Oed.   I agree and have already done something about it. Right after Creon delivered the oracle's message he told me I should send for Tiresias, and I have—twice, in fact. I expect him any minute now.   31

Sen.   The curses you have called down upon the murderer should certainly make him quake with fear!

Oed.   I doubt it. A person who does wicked deeds probably won't be scared by words.

Sen.   Then we need to find him and do something. Here's the man that can expose him—the prophet, the man who does not lie.

(The blind prophet Tiresias enters, led by a boy.)

Oed.   Tiresias, you search out everything in heaven and earth, named and nameless. You can't see the city but you're aware of our plague. And now you're the only one who can help us. For Apollo—if you haven't already heard about this—sent word by the oracle that we wouldn't have any release from this land's sickness till we had found the man, or men, that killed Laius, and either killed them or drove them out of the country. Therefore, we need you to tell us what you can determine, using whatever prophetic gifts you can. Save yourself, save the city, save me. At this point we are like an infected body. We ask you for healing.   43

Tir.   Alas! How terrible it is to know when knowing doesn't do one any good. I was well aware of the plague situation, of course, but I have not chosen to come forth.

Oed.   Why not? How can you be so heartless?

Tir.   Just let me go home. That's the easiest way you can bear your burden. That's my counsel.

Oed.   You have not spoken like a loyal son of the state that gave you life, or even like a friend to the state, cheating us of your response.

Tir.   That's because I see the outcome.   50

Oed.   For heaven's sake, if you have knowledge, do not hold it back. All of us are begging you!

Tir.   That's because you don't have my knowledge. I won't have my say, because it will bring your sorrow into display.

Oed.   What, you know something, and won't tell it? You are willing to betray us and destroy the city?

Tir.   I will not bring remorse upon myself and upon you. Why do you have to search these matters out? Forget it; I won't tell.

Oed.   Worst of traitors! You would arouse a stone to wrath. Are you going to say anything, or not?

Tir.   You condemn me—yet your own offense, in your house, you don't even see. Instead you get mad at me!   61

Oed.   Who wouldn't take offense, hearing you betray your own city?

Tir.   Well, what is going to happen will happen, but I don't want to be involved.

Oed.   What is it that's going to come, that you're so committed to keeping your mouth shut about?

Tir.   My mouth will stay shut. Storm if you please, feel free to rage.

Oed.　　　I am in a rage, but at least in my rage I don't spare any details that are clear to me. You know, now it's becoming clear to me. I believe you're trying to keep quiet because you were in on the plot to kill Laius. I believe you actually worked it out—everything but the actual killing with your own hands. If you weren't blind, I'd suspect you did it all by yourself!　　　　　　　　　　　　　　　　　　　　70

Tir.　　　Is that so? All right, I charge you to abide by the decree you proclaimed. From this time on don't speak to me or anyone else in this city—since you yourself are the pollution of this land!

Oed.　　　You think you can say something like that, in public, and go free?

Tir.　　　I am free. I am freely speaking the truth.

Oed.　　　Who got you to say this?

Tir.　　　You did! You made me speak it against my will.

Oed.　　　What was it you said again?

Tir.　　　Why? Didn't you understand it the first time?

Oed.　　　I simply can't believe my ears. Say it more clearly.　　80

Tir.　　　You are Laius' murderer; you are the man you seek.

Oed.　　　You will be severely punished for saying something like that.

Tir.　　　How would you like to hear something else, that will make you even madder?

Oed.　　　Everything you say is a waste of time.

Tir.　　　You live in shame with those closest to you. You don't see the evilness in which you abide.

Oed.　　　Do you really think you can get away with stuff like this?

Tir.　　　Yes, if truth has any power.

Oed.　　　Truth does have power, but you don't; you're blind in your eyes, and in your ears, and in your mind.　　　　　　90

Tir.　　　You're blaming me, but very soon all these people around are going to be blaming you.

Oed.   You can't hurt me. Physically and mentally, you live in night.

Tir.   Apollo will bring everything to pass. I don't need to do anything.

Oed.   Say—are these accusations something you came up with, or did you get your ideas from Creon?

Tir.   Your blame doesn't come from Creon, but from your own self.

Oed.   Ah. This is all about riches, and power, and craftiness. When I came along, this state was committed to my keeping, without my even coming here to obtain it. Now Creon, my relative, my friend— I thought—has figured out a way to undermine my authority, to take all this away from me, and he has used this sorcerer to do it. This "prophet" doesn't have eyes for anything but gold. Tell me something: if you're supposed to be so smart about everything, how come when the Sphinx came along, you didn't use your superior knowledge to set this people free? They could have used some words of wisdom then. But you didn't have any. No one did, till I came along, plain old Oedipus, without a fancy religious education, and I ended the power of the Sphinx simply by using my wits. And now you're trying to get me thrown out of the country, hoping to be next to the throne of a new king! You're going to be sorry for this, believe me.

Sen.   My lord, speaking for all of us, we think that his words and yours have both merely been displays of anger, and that's not what we need right now. What we need is this: to consider how best to inter-pret the oracle of Apollo.   109

Tir. (to Oedipus) You may be the king, but at least we are equals in being able to put together an argument. First, I am the servant of Apollo, not Creon. Second, since you've brought up my blindness and mocked me with it, let me respond: You have your sight, yet you can't see the evils around you, nor even know who you live with, or whose house you're living in. Do you even know who you come from? No, you're totally ignorant to all that. But some day soon this land will drive you away, from the curse of your father and mother, with eyes that will be blind then, though they look around so proudly now. What place on earth will be a shelter for you at that time? Go ahead—trample on Creon, trample on me. But know this: no one on earth is going to be bruised more than you.

Oed.   How much more of this do I have to listen to? To hell with you! Get out of here!

Tir.   You were the one that called me. I didn't want to come here in the first place   120

Oed.   I didn't know you were going to talk such stupidity.

Tir.   You may think I'm foolish, but your father, who brought you into this world, thought I was wise.

Oed.   What father? Stop! Who do you think my father is?

Tir.   Today will provide you with birth and death at the same time.

Oed.   Everything you say is just one stupid riddle after another.

Tir.   Well, aren't you supposed to be the big riddle-solver?

Oed.   At least I could save the city by solving a riddle.

Tir.   Well, I am going. Boy, take me home.

Oed.   Yes, get lost. Your ignorant words just get us off the track. When you are gone, you can't annoy us any more.   131

Tir.   Well, I have said my say. I'm not afraid of you, so I'll repeat one last time: The man you have been seeking and threatening is right here. He is thought sighted and wealthy, but he'll soon be blind and poor. He'll need a stick to walk with. To his own sons he'll be discovered to be both brother and father, and to his own wife he'll be son and spouse. He is his own father, and he has murdered his own father. Go inside and ponder what I have said. If you detect me in a lie, then come arrest me as a false prophet.

SCENE 3

Creon enters to speak to the senators.

Cre.   Fellow citizens, I have come here because I have heard that King Oedipus is making terrible accusations against me that I will not put up with. If he thinks I have said or done anything to harm him in any way, I'd rather not live a life in which I am considered a traitor in this town. Having one's reputation destroyed is not a trifle. I don't want to be called a criminal here in my hometown, especially by my friends, such as all of you.

Sen.   Well, we really think he said those things just because he was mad, rather than from really thinking it through.

Cre.   But I've been told that Oedipus said the prophet lied, and that I was the one who told him to.

Sen.   The prophet said the things you've probably heard; how he came up with them, I don't know. But here comes Oedipus from the palace; you can ask what he thinks.   11

(Oedipus enters.)

Oed.   (seeing Creon) How did you dare come here? Have you been boasting about your daring, how you were able to spend time with me all these years, setting me up for the final blow? Do you think I'm a coward or a fool, that you thought you could get away with this scheme? Did you think I couldn't recognize your hand in this, or that I couldn't defend myself? Isn't it foolish for you to think you can take over a throne without a group of followers?

Cre.   Do me a favor. Let me speak, and see if you can learn something.

Oed.   I don't have anything to learn from you.

Cre. If you suppose that arrogance counts for more than reason, you are far wrong.

Oed. If you suppose you can escape punishment due murder, you are far wrong!   20

Cre. Fair enough. But tell me: Why have you told people I have harmed you?

Oed. Did you tell me to send for that damned prophet, or not?

Cre. I did, and I still think it was good advice.

Oed. How long is it since Laius died?

Cre. I'm not sure, exactly—maybe a couple of decades.

Oed. Was this so-called seer around then?

Cre. Yes, and just as highly respected then as now.

Oed. Did he at that time say one single word about me?

Cre. Not while I was ever around.

Oed. Did you investigate Laius' case at all?   30

Cre. A little, but there wasn't any evidence.

Oed. Okay. So why didn't this bigmouth have anything to say about me back then?

Cre. That I don't know. And when I don't know something I don't give an answer about it.

Oed. But there's one thing you do know.

Cre. What's that?

Oed. That prophet would never have said I was the one who murdered Laius without having you to back him up!

Cre. You know more about what Tiresias has said than I do. But now it's my turn to interrogate.

Oed. Ask whatever you want. But nobody's going to pin this murder on me.   40

Cre. Okay. My sister is your wife, right?

Oed. Nobody denies that.

Cre. Together you rule all of Thebes and the outlying areas?

Oed. She gets everything she wants from me.

Cre.   And am I not so close to the two of you that it's like being your equal?

Oed.   Why, yes—that's the damned shame of it all!   46

Cre.   Not if you think about it the way I have. Consider this: I currently have all the power of full access to the king with no kingly worries. I don't want to be a king; why should I, when I already have kingly wealth and power? Nobody with any sense would try something like you're talking about. Right now, when I want anything, I ask you for it and get it. I'd have those things if I were king, true, but I'd also have a lot of responsibilities that I don't really want to deal with. Why would a throne be any better than painless authority? Right now, I'm one of the most popular, important people in the whole country. Everybody greets me; people do favors for me and act nice to me. They all know I'm their hope of getting something from you if they ever need it. Now why would I give all this up for a crime? In fact, if someone suggested an idea like this to me, I'd throw them out. You want proof? Go to Pytho yourself. Ask what Apollo's oracle said, and see whether I quoted accurately. If you find out I'm a liar, or if you get any evidence that I'm in league with Tiresias against you, then take my life—I'll even vote for my death then myself! But do not, on the basis of some dubious argument that you've come up with in your head, charge me without any facts. It's wrong to decide bad men are good or to decide good men are bad. You might as well get rid of your own life as to turn away a trustworthy friend. Oh, well; in time you'll see everything plainly. Time, and time alone, can show that a man is honest; but in one day you can determine whether a man is evil.   63

Sen.   His words sound right, my lord; perhaps you should not act too swiftly.

Oed.   When a person plots swiftly against me in the dark, I have to act swiftly to protect myself. If I stay quiet, my enemy wins.

Cre.   What do you want? Me expelled from the country?

Oed.   No. I should have you killed.

Cre.   What!

Oed.   You are a traitor.   70

Cre.   You're not a judge.

Oed.   But I'm the ruler.

Cre.   You're ruling badly.

Oed.   This is my city.

Cre.   And my city, too.

Sen.   Good lords, here comes Jocasta, and in good time. She's coming from the palace.

Perhaps with her help the two of you can settle your differences.

(Jocasta enters.)

Joc.   Unhappy men, what made you raise your voices so loud? Why this senseless broil of words? Aren't you ashamed to air private quarrels when the land is so afflicted? Oedipus, come inside. Creon, please go home. Don't turn something small into a public brawl.   80

Cre.   Sister, your husband Oedipus thinks it's right to treat me villainously. He's trying to decide between two bad things: whether to kill me, or just throw me out of the country.

Oed.   I admit it, wife; for I have found him treacherously plotting against me.

Cre.   May heaven never allow me to thrive if I have done a single thing of what you charge me with!

Joc.   Oedipus! In heaven's name believe him! Respect Creon's word, and respect his oath.

Sen.   Listen to her, my king. With goodwill toward you I encourage you to listen.

Oed.   About what?

Sen.   Respect his word. Creon has always been a man of his word, and this is a weighty oath he has backed it up with.   90

Oed.   Do you know what you're asking?

Sen.   Yes.

Oed.   Then say it.

Sen.   I'm asking that you not ever expel, with disgrace, a friend when you lack proof.

Oed.   No. If you ask me to respect his word, what you're really asking is this—that I be killed or exiled!

Sen.   No! Absolutely not! May heaven let me perish to the uttermost if I mean any harm to you. But this quarrel between our leaders, with all the other troubles of the land, is just too much.

Oed.   All right. Let him go, even though I get killed outright, or thrust by force, dishonored, from the land. Your voice, not his, makes me compassionate. Wherever Creon goes, he shall have my hatred.   101

Cre.   Even when you yield you show your pettiness.

Oed.   Leave me! Get out of here!

Cre.   I'm going. You don't know me; these honest people here do. (Creon leaves.)

Joc.   How did all this get started?

Oed.   It was all Creon's fault. He's been plotting against me.

Joc.   In what way?

Oed.   He says I killed Laius.

Joc.   Why? Has he heard something, or does he say he knows this?

Oed.   No, it comes from the words of that stupid prophet. 110

Joc.   Is that all? Listen to me: Soothsayers don't know what they're talking about. Let me prove it to you. Once a long time ago a message came to Laius through an oracle. I don't mean the message was from Apollo himself, but from the prophets that claim to speak for him. The message said that Laius would die by the hand of his own son, a son from my own womb. But actually Laius was killed by robbers, not far from here, at a place where three roads meet. And our son couldn't have done it because at the age of only three days, Laius pierced his ankles and had servants take him out into a lonely wasteland to die. So the baby did not grow up to be his father's murderer, and Laius did not get killed by his own son, which the oracle had made him afraid of. This is how much knowledge soothsayers have of the future. So there's no need for you to get worked up about anything a prophet says.   120

Oed.   What fear comes upon me, wife, hearing you talk!

Joc.   Why? What's the matter?

Oed.   I thought I heard you say Laius was killed at a place where three roads meet.

Joc.   That's right.

Oed.   Where is that spot located?

Joc.   Over near Phocis. Roads from here, Daulia, and Delphi converge there.

Oed.   How long ago was this?

Joc.   We heard the news—well, it was shortly before you came to Thebes.

Oed.   God of heaven! What are you doing to me!

Joc.   Oedipus, what is it?   130

Oed.   Don't ask me yet. Laius—what was he like? About how old?

Joc.   He was tall, with the first few touches of white in his hair. Built about like you.

Oed.   Miserable! I've cursed myself without even knowing it!

Joc.   What are you saying? Oedipus, you're scaring me!

Oed.   I am scared to death that prophet was a true seer after all. But you'll make me certain, if you answer one thing more.

Joc.   I'm trembling, but I'll answer it.

Oed.   Was Laius traveling the way a king usually does, with an armed guard of soldiers, or was he poorly attended?

Joc.   Only five people, including Laius.   140

Oed.   O, I see it all! Woman, who gave you this information?

Joc.   A servant, the only one of the five who escaped when it happened.

Oed.   Is he by any chance still living in the house?

Joc.   No. He came back, but then when he saw you were named the new king, he came to me—that very day, I believe—and said he had always wanted to be a shepherd on his own, and he begged me for permission to leave the palace and go out as a field worker. He said he was afraid people in town would always identify him with the death of the king.

He had been an excellent servant for years, and I could understand his feelings, so I let him go.

Oed.   How quickly can we get him here?

Joc.   Within a day, I suppose, if we had to. But why?   150

Oed.   Wife, I'm almost afraid I've said too much already.

Joc.   We'll have the man come here right away. But I think I deserve to know what it is that's weighing on you so heavily.

Oed.   I will tell you. Who can I tell something this significant to, if not to you? Okay. As you know, my father and mother are Polybus and Merope, the king and queen of Corinth. Being their son, I was naturally one of the leading citizens there. Then one day something happened—perhaps not that important, but it really bothered me. One day at a tavern a man who had had too much to drink said that I didn't really belong to my parents. I wondered what he meant, whether there was anything to it. Was I illegitimate? And so the next day I confronted my parents about it. They said it was just a scandal and got really mad at the drunk for saying something like that. So I felt better, but still—it seemed that the story had spread around through a bunch of the old-timers. So without telling my father or mother where I was going, I set out for Pytho, to visit the oracle of Apollo. Apollo wouldn't answer my question about what the drunk said, but there were other things revealed—strange and terrible things. The oracle said I would kill my father and marry my mother! Well, when I heard that, I immediately thought, *I've got to keep this from happening.* So I decided on the spot to make myself an exile from Corinth, to be so far away that I wouldn't have to worry about the prophecy coming true. As I journeyed away from Corinth, looking for a place to settle down, I came to a place where three roads meet, the place where, you tell me now, Laius died. My wife, I'll tell you the whole story. As I was traveling down the road, there came from the other direction a man riding in a small carriage, looking just the way you described Laius. The carriage-driver swung too far toward me and nearly knocked me down. I got mad and hit the driver, and when this man riding in the carriage saw that, he hit me on the head with a stick. That did it! I took my staff, jumped into the carriage, killed him, and threw him out. I killed all of them I could get my hands on. If that man in the carriage was Laius, then I am now the most miserable man in the whole world. Nobody can have me in their house again, nobody can greet me, everybody has to throw me out. And I pronounced the curses myself! Am I not vile and unclean? I can never see my family again, never set foot in my native land, or else I might kill my father Polybus and marry my mother. And now this! I might as well leave behind the sight of humanity forever.   179

Sen.   My lord, we are all grieving for you. Still, until we hear the story from that one survivor, we shouldn't lose all hope.

Oed.   Yes. That shepherd is indeed my one piece of hope.

Joc.   I've sent for him already. But how can that shepherd help you?

Oed.   Like this: If he tells the story the way you said he did, I'm free and clear.

Joc.   Why? What doesn't match up?

Oed.   You told me he said "robbers" killed Laius—plural. If he swears that it was indeed multiple people who killed Laius, then it wasn't me; I must have killed someone else. One is not the same as many. But if he admits that one person killed four, then it's obvious that I'm guilty.

Joc.   Oh, I remember it quite well; he plainly said "robbers." He can't take it back now; the whole city heard it! But even if he does shift from his story, that still doesn't explain the prophecy about the death of Laius. He still wasn't killed by our son. The poor baby couldn't have killed him because it died before it turned a week old! So like I said before, don't bother worrying about the predictions of soothsayers.   193

Oed.   That's a good point. Still, I want to see this shepherd.

SCENE 4

A messenger comes up to Jocasta and the senators.

Mess.   Excuse me. Can any of you tell me where Oedipus the king lives? Or even better, do you know where he is right now?

Sen.   Stranger, right here behind us is where he lives, and he's inside at the moment. This lady here is his wife.

Mess.   Blessings be on you, Ma'am.

Joc.   And the same to you, Sir. What have you come here for?

Mess.   I've come to bring good news to you and your husband.

Joc.   From where?

Mess.   From Corinth. Well, actually it's good news mixed with bad, so you'll probably feel some sadness about it. But I hope overall the news brings you pleasure.   10

Joc.   What is it? What sort of news can be so ambiguous?

Mess.   The people in the land of Corinth want Oedipus to come back and be their king.

Joc.   What! What happened to Polybus?

Mess.   He's dead and in the grave.

Joc.   Seriously? Polybus is dead?

Mess.   Ma'am, I'm not telling you a lie.

Joc.   Someone go tell Oedipus instantly! Prophecies, where is your power now? Oedipus ran away from this man so long ago, stayed away so many years, afraid of killing him, and now he dies without Oedipus even being around!

(Oedipus enters.)

Oed.   What is it, Jocasta? What did you want to see me about? 20
Joc.   Listen to this man! Hear what the cloudy sayings of the gods have come to.
Oed.   Who is he? What does he have to say?
Joc.   He's from Corinth, and he says your father Polybus is dead!
Oed.   Sir, is that true?
Mess.   Yes. Polybus has gone the way of all mortals.
Oed.   Was it by treason, or disease, or what?
Mess.   He simply died of old age; the man was up in years.
Oed.   Hurrah! Wife, why do people bother paying any attention to oracles? They said I was going to kill my father! He's dead, clear out of sight, and here I am, having nothing at all to do with it! Unless—maybe they mean that he pined away from grief when I never returned, and so I killed him that way. But after 20 years—no way! Polybus is gone, and so as far as I'm concerned you can take all oracles and send them to hell forever!   32
Joc.   Isn't this just what I've been saying the whole time?
Oed.   You did. But—I was just so afraid.
Joc.   Well, now you can finally get all these stupid predictions off your mind.
Oed.   Yet—I'm still afraid of being in my mother's bed.
Joc.   Why should men be afraid, when nobody can predict the future? It's best just to live your life as it comes. As for that thing of having sex with your mother, don't worry about that. Lots of men at some point dream about having sex with their mothers. But it's just a dream—don't worry about it.   40

Oed.   Well, I hear what you're saying, and I want to believe it, but I will still have this sense of dread as long as my mother is alive.

Mess.   What woman is this you're so afraid of?

Oed.   Merope, Polybus' wife.

Mess.   What are you afraid of about her?

Oed.   A dark oracle from heaven.

Mess.   Do you mind telling me what it said?

Oed.   No, not at all. The oracle declared that one day I would marry my mother and kill my father with my own hands. That prophecy was the reason I left Corinth and have stayed away all these years. I've prospered here in Thebes; still, there's heartache in never getting to see your parents again.   51

Mess.   You mean this prophecy was why you left Corinth?

Oed.   Sure; I didn't want to kill my father.

Mess.   Well, I came here to give you one piece of good news, and I didn't realize I would be giving you two!

Oed.   What do you mean? If you can ease my fears I will certainly reward you for it.

Mess.   I must confess, this is why I asked to be the one delivering the news. I was hopeful that when you become king of Corinth you might remember how I took the trouble to travel to you.

Oed.   That's labor lost, because I will never travel to Corinth while either parent is living.

Mess.   Sir, it's obvious that you still don't know who you are.   60

Oed.   What? What are you talking about?

Mess.   You were afraid of killing your father, right?

Oed.   Yes, deathly afraid.

Mess.   You really didn't have a single thing to worry about.

Oed.   How could that be, if I stayed around Polybus?

Mess.   Because Polybus was not related to you at all!

Oed.   What!

Mess.   Why, I'm just as much related to you as Polybus was!

Oed.   But you're not—how could my father not be related to me?

Mess.   Because he wasn't your father.   70

Oed.   Then why did he always call me his son?

Mess.   Because I gave you to him—as a gift!

Oed.   He loved me that much?

Mess.   Yes, because he had gone so long without being able to have children.

Oed.   Did you find me or buy me, to give to him?

Mess.   I picked you up in the woods near here.

Oed.   What were you doing in these parts?

Mess.   I used to be a shepherd in the hills around here.

Oed.   A paid shepherd?

Mess.   Yes. And I was your life preserver!   80

Oed.   Why? What danger was I in?

Mess.   I see your ankles still look a bit sore and red.

Oed.   What's that old injury got to do with anything?

Mess.   At the time I untied you, both your ankles had holes pierced in them.

Oed.   Who could have done something like that to me?

Mess.   That I don't know. The person who gave you to me would know more about that than I would.

Oed.   You didn't find me yourself, then.

Mess.   No, another shepherd gave you to me.

Oed.   Who? Would you still recognize him?   90

Mess.   They said he was a servant for Laius, helping out with the herds.

Oed.   You mean the Laius who used to be king here?

Mess.   Exactly. This man was herding sheep for him at the time.

Oed.   And is that shepherd still alive?

Mess.   Well, you folks would know more about that than I would. After all, you live around here; I don't.

Oed.   Do any of you people know this servant he's talking about, the guy who used to herd sheep for Laius?

Sen.   I think he's probably talking about the same shepherd that you're already trying to get to come here. Jocasta probably knows whether it would be the same man.   100

Oed.   Jocasta, what do you think? Would it be the same person?

Joc.   Why, what difference does it make? Don't worry about it.

Oed.   But I've got a clue! I might be close to figuring out who my real parents are.

Joc.   For heaven's sake, if you care about me at all, or if you care about yourself, don't pursue this any further! Can't you see I'm starting to feel sick over all this talk?

Oed.   Have courage, wife. Even if it turns out my parents were slaves, that can't hurt us any at this point.

Joc.   I'm begging you not to explore this further.

Oed.   I'm so close, I've got to do it now.   109

Joc.   Wretched man! Everything is ruined, everything! That is my final word to you, forever!

(She leaves.)

Sen.   Why did she run off, Oedipus? Why did she seem so filled with grief? I'm afraid of what might come out of all this.

Oed.   Whatever comes, I won't hesitate. But here's what I suspect. She's always thought I came from a royal family. She's a proud woman, and now it's possible I come from a really low-class family. Well, I don't care who my family is!

SCENE 5

A shepherd enters to talk with Oedipus, the senators, and the messenger.

Oed.   Here comes a man dressed like a shepherd. I imagine this is the one we've been talking about; his old age about matches with this messenger's.

Sen.   Yes, this man used to be a servant of Laius', and he did a good bit of shepherding in those days.

Oed.   Corinthian stranger, is this the man you were talking about?

Mess.   Yes, that's the one.

Oed.   Old man, I have some questions for you. Did you used to belong to Laius?

Shep.   Yes, a long time ago.

Oed.   What sort of work did you do for him?

Shep.   Various things, but perhaps more taking care of sheep than anything else.   10

Oed.   Where did you do this?

Shep.   Mostly in the Cithaeron Hills area.

Oed.   (indicating messenger) Have you ever seen this man before? Did you know him back then?

Shep.   No, I don't think so. Not as far as I can recall, anyway.

Mess.   Well, that's not too surprising; it was a long time ago. But I can remind him. Sir, remember in the Cithaeron Hills area, between here and Corinth, we were on ground next to each other for three summers? You had two flocks, I had one. In the winter you brought your flocks back to the stables of Laius, and I always took mine to some pens on the other side of the hills. Remember that?   20

Shep.   Yes, it's starting to come back to me now. That was an awfully long time ago.

Mess.   Okay. Do you remember the day that you had that baby boy with you, and you handed him to me, and said I could do whatever I wanted to with him?

Shep.   What are you asking me about that for?

Mess.   Because right here is the baby you saved!

Shep.   Shut up!

Oed.   Old man, don't talk to this stranger like that; you need to learn manners.

Shep.   What have I done to hurt anybody?

Oed.   You're holding back information on that baby he's talking about.

Shep.   He doesn't know what he's talking about! He's crazy! 30

Oed.   If you won't talk of your own free will, we'll make you talk.

Shep.   Please don't hurt me. I'm an old man.

Oed.   Quick, somebody twist his arms behind his back till he starts talking.

Shep.   I'll talk! What do you want to know?

Oed.   Did you give him that boy baby he's talking about?

Shep.   I did. I wish I had died instead.

Oed.   If you don't tell us the total truth, you'll get your wish today.

Shep.   But if I speak, you'll be even madder at me.

Oed.   I don't believe this old man wants to tell us anything. Perhaps if you guards apply more pressure....   40

Shep.   No! No! Stop! I said I did it! I gave him the baby, a long time ago.

Oed.   Where did you get this baby from?

Shep.   It wasn't mine; I got it from somebody else.

Oed.   Who? Where did it come from?

Shep.   Don't, Master, for God's sake please don't ask me that question!

Oed. If I have to ask you again, you're a dead man.

Shep. All right. The baby came from Laius' house.

Oed. Was it a slave? Or from his own family?

Shep. O, Sir, I'm at the point of saying something horrible!

Oed. And I'm at the point of hearing something horrible. But I have to hear it anyway.   50

Shep. Well, I understood it to be Laius' own son. But your wife can best answer that question.

Oed. Was she the one who gave the baby to you?

Shep. My lord, yes.

Oed. For what purpose?

Shep. She said I was supposed to make sure it didn't live.

Oed. And she was its mother? That's awful!

Shep. Well, they were afraid of an evil prophecy.

Oed. What prophecy?

Shep. That the baby was supposed to kill its father.

Oed. So why did you give the baby to this man here? 60

Shep. Oh, sir, I felt sorry for that baby! I thought he would just get it out of my sight, but he actually saved the baby! And it's a tragedy, because if you're that baby, you're a man born for misery!

Oed. Pain! Pain! I see the whole thing now. Light, this is the last time I'll ever see you again.

Because I have been revealed as the man who married his—and the man who killed his—Horrible! (He rushes into the palace.)

SCENE 6

A palace guard comes out to the senators.

Guar. O you the honored leaders of this land, what sights you have to see, what deeds you have to hear, if you care about the household of Laius. The mightiest river could not purge this house of all the evil doings it contains. It's an infected house, a wounded house.

Sen.   We had enough to grieve about already; what more is there now?

Mess.   It won't take long to relate. Our beloved Jocasta is no more.

Sen.   Poor lady! What happened?   6

Mess.   Suicide. You're being spared the saddest part by not having to look at it. But I will tell you what happened. When she came running into the house she was crying frantically. She went straight to the bedroom, pulling on her hair, shutting the doors behind her. She kept crying out the name of Laius, crying about the baby, crying about having sex with the baby, crying about having children by her own son. Then it got quiet. After a little while into the house stormed Oedipus, yelling for somebody to get him a sword, asking where he could find his wife. He was raving like a lunatic. We were all afraid to say anything. He decided to check the bedroom, so he beat open the doors. There we found his wife, dangling, a noose around her neck. When he saw her, he groaned and went to her, taking her down and removing the noose. He stretched her out on the floor. Then what followed next was just terrible, absolutely horrifying. Jocasta had two gold pins on her dress as decorations. Oedipus took the pins and stabbed them into his own eyeballs. He yelled something about they were never going to see evil again. He stabbed those eyes over and over, blood running down his face, not drop by drop, but pouring down in two streams. They used to be so happy together! And now nothing is left, nothing but death and shame.   21

Sen.   How is he now?

Guar.   He's calling for someone to lead him outside, someone to show all of Thebes the father-killer, the mother—I can't say what he said. He says he's going to throw himself out of the land. Really, it's more than you can bear. But see for yourself; I see him groping his way out here toward us.

(Oedipus enters, blind and wounded.)

Oed.   So miserable! Where can I go now?

Sen.   How could you do this to yourself?

Oed.   It was Apollo, Apollo did all—no, I am the one who brought this on myself. And why would I ever want to see again? What delight can be left for me? The gods hate me. Someone lead me into exile.   31

Sen.   I would think death would be better than living in blindness.

Oed.   No more advice. Don't try to tell me now that you think I didn't do the best thing. How could I ever go to the afterlife and look on the face of my father? How could I look my mother in the eyes? I sinned against both of them, and deserve more than death. Do you think I would have any joy in seeing my children again? Kill me, or send me away, whatever you think best.

Sen.   Creon is coming; we'll let him decide what to do. He's the only adult member of your family left to protect the land.

Oed.   What can I possibly say to him? I was totally wrong about him!   39

(Creon enters.)

Cre.   Oedipus, I haven't come here to make your misery any worse. And I haven't come to reproach you for the pain you caused me. But let's not parade our family miseries out in public any more. Get inside the house; that's the decent thing to do.

Oed.   Please say first that you'll do me one favor.

Cre.   What's that?

Oed.   Get me out of this country as quickly as possible.

Cre.   I would have already started to bring that about, except that I wanted to check with the gods first, to see how they want things handled.

Oed.   Surely the oracle was already clear!

Cre.   It seemed so. But this is an important matter; we want to be sure at each step that we are doing the right thing.   50

Oed.   You want to consult the gods about a wretch like me?

Cre.   I think you have learned that we can trust the gods. Now go.

(Oedipus goes inside.)

Sen.   Dwellers in Thebes, behold the life of Oedipus: The man who solved the riddle, our prince, whom everyone looked up to and envied. Now see how the billows of calamity roll over him. Let no one ever say about any person, "He has a fortunate life," until that life has completely, and safely, ended.

ANTIGONE

◆

By Sophocles (c. 445 B.C.)
(Translated by George Young, contemporized and abridged
by Dr. Marv Hinten)

CHARACTERS

Creon, King of Thebes
Antigone, Creon's niece
Ismene, her sister
Haemon, Creon's son, Antigone's fiancé
Tiresias, a blind prophet
Eurydice, Creon's wife
A soldier
A messenger
Senator, part of the chorus (Theban senators)

BACKGROUND: Oedipus, after blinding himself, leaves Thebes. His son Eteocles is chosen the new ruler of Thebes. This makes Eteocles' older brother Polynices mad; he thought that as Oedipus' older son, he should have been made ruler. So Polynices raises an army and attacks Thebes; in the battle, he and Eteocles kill each other. Now that the battle has ended, their uncle, Creon, is the new ruler. He decrees that Eteocles will be buried with full honors but that Polynices, as a traitor, will be left out on the ground to rot. The play begins with Antigone and Ismene, the daughters of Oedipus and Jocasta, horrified that one of their brothers will be left unburied; to the Greeks, this sort of disrespect for the dead seemed to insult the gods as well.

SCENE 1

Setting: Morning, in front of the Theban royal palace. Antigone and Ismene are talking.

Ant.   Ismene, dear sister, can you tell how heaven means to bring upon the two of us before we die all the ills that come from the life of Oedipus? We have undergone sorrow and harm, scandal and shame. And now, have you heard the latest?

Isme.   Antigone, I haven't heard anything of importance, positive or negative, since we lost both our brothers, both in the same day, each killing the other. And since the attacking army lost and left, I haven't heard of anything else that would make me either happier or more miserable.

Ant.   I thought so. That's why I had you come here; I wanted to talk with you privately.

Isme.   What is it? What's the big mystery?   8

Ant.   Well. Creon is allowing one of our brothers to be entombed, covered from sight, and the other brother he is only covering with insults. Eteocles has been buried with the honored dead, as the law requires. But as for the dead body of Polynices, this is the public proclamation: No one can go out and weep over it; no one can bury it; it's to be left for the buzzards. This is the statement of the high-and-mighty Creon. And he's telling everyone that he really means this. Anyone who breaks this law must die, stoned to death by the citizens in the streets. So stands the case. Now it's time for you to show whether you are really of noble birth, or not.

Isme.   If this is the way it is, what can I do about it, either way?

Ant.   Look, will you join me? Will you work with me?

Isme.   To do what? What are you talking about?

Ant.   Help me lift the body—

Isme.   What?! Are you thinking about burying him? Against the proclamation?   20

Ant.   He's our brother; of course I'm planning to bury him! Whether you help or not, I'll do it; I won't prove disloyal.

Isme.   You're mad! When Creon has forbidden it?

Ant.   He doesn't have any right to keep me from my brother.

Isme.   O sister, think how our father perished! He was abhorred—dishonored—blind—his eyes put out by his own hand! Remember how Jocasta, his wife and mother at the same time, ended her own life with a knotted noose! Remember how our two brothers destroyed each other on the same day! And now it's just the two of us. How miserably do you think the two of us will die if we try to trample on the power of the king? Keep in mind that we are mere women, not able to cope with men; we are ruled by those mightier than ourselves. For my part, I plan to ask forgiveness from the dead for the things I'm being forced to do. I have to yield obedience to the powerful; anything else would be madness, not wisdom.   32

Ant.   Well, I'll never ask you to help me with anything again. Even if you wanted to help me now I wouldn't let you. Do whatever seems right to you; I'm going to bury our brother. Death brought on by the capital crime of holiness would be an honor. Loving and loved, I will someday lie by my brother's side. I have to satisfy the powers below the earth far longer than the powers on the earth; for I will lie below the earth forever. As for you, you can feel free to scorn what heaven approves.

Isme.   I am not one to cover things with scorn; but I am too feeble to fight against the state.

Ant.   Yes, keep on saying that; but I will heap a burial mound over my most dear brother.

Isme.   Poor sister. I fear for you so much!   41

Ant.   Don't waste your fear on me. Steer your own course.

Isme.　　　At least don't tell anybody what you're planning to do. You can count on me to keep your secret.

Ant.　　　Tell it, tell it! Rather than you keeping silent, I'd prefer you tell the whole world!

Isme.　　　How can you be this way?

Ant.　　　I have the approval of the ones I most need to please.

Isme.　　　Perhaps so, if you could actually do it. But you're wanting to do the impossible.

Ant.　　　When I no longer have the power to move, I will stop trying.

Isme.　　　If something's impossible, it's wrong to even try.　　50

Ant.　　　If you keep saying that, I'm going to start despising you, and our dead brother will hate you. Allow me my piece of "foolishness," if you like; I'm willing to meet what is threatened.

The very worst that can happen to me is death with honor.

Isme.　　　If your mind's made up, then go, and take this with you: You're going on a fool's errand! But I must admit, you're true to your beloved brother.

SCENE 2

King Creon is meeting with the senate of Thebes.

Cre.　　　Sirs, the ship of state has rocked in stormy seas, but the gods have set her on an even keel once more. Therefore I have summoned you here, since you have always been loyal, during both the time of Oedipus and the recent uprisings. Now the brothers are dead and, as Oedipus' nearest living male kin, I have taken the throne and the power. What are my views of laws and government? I have no respect for anyone who puts a friend above his native land. If I see evil marching toward my country I will not sit quietly by; and if I see someone act as an enemy toward my city, I cannot count him as my friend. And so I have given orders to the citizens regarding the sons of Oedipus. Eteocles fought defending the city, and so I ordered that he be given full burial rights. Meanwhile, his brother Polynices—who tried to burn down his native city—who fought against his native gods—who tried to kill his own flesh and blood—I have had proclaimed throughout the city that no one should bury him, no one should mourn him; his body is to be left for the vultures and wild dogs. Such is my will. As long as I am king, we honor the righteous, but not the wicked.   13

    Sen.   And what do you want from us?

    Cre.   Not to support disobedience.

    Sen.   No one is foolish enough to embrace death.

    Cre.   Death is indeed the penalty. But men often have dreams of gain that bring them to ruin.

(A soldier enters.)

    Sol.   My lord, I came here because I felt it my duty, but I kept thinking to myself, *Is this really a good idea?* But then every time I started to turn back, I thought, *What if Creon hears about this from somebody else?* So I hurried here, but by fits and starts.   20

    Cre.   What are you talking about?

    Sol.   First let me tell you my role in all this. I didn't do the deed, I didn't see it done, and so I don't think I should suffer in any way for what somebody else did.

    Cre.   Nice job of building yourself a wall of protection. But clearly you have something to tell?

    Sol.   Yes. Something serious.

    Cre.   OK. Start telling your story, then finish it, then leave.

    Sol.   I am telling you. That body we were watching—someone has buried it, sort of. They sprinkled dust on it, added some coverings, and took off.

    Cre.   What? What man dared to do this?   29

Sol. I have no idea. There were no footprints or wheelprints. The first sentry to get out there to the body after your proclamation discovered that someone had poured dust on the body.

Everybody blamed everybody else for being too slow to get there. We all swore we didn't have anything to do with it. Finally one man said, "Somebody has to tell Creon about this." We cast lots, and I was the loser, and not very happy about it either—nobody likes a messenger who brings bad news.

Sen. My lord, do you think the gods had anything to do with this?

Cre. Shut up before you get me mad! Fool! To think that the gods care about this dead body.

Would they want to honor someone who came in to set fire to their city? Do the gods honor evil? No, right from the start some people didn't like the proclamation, and they've paid off the sentries to do this. Well, the sentries may have been paid, but now I'll make them pay! You, deliver this message to your fellow sentries: If you people don't bring back to me the person who did this outrage, you'll get not only death but more besides! I'll teach all of you that greed doesn't pay. 43

Sol. May I say something?

Cre. Can't you see I don't want you around?

Sol. It's terrible when a man is suspicious, and the suspicion is false.

Cre. Live with it. Let me know who did this, or you'll soon find out the money you received wasn't worth it. (He leaves.)

Sol. I hope the person does get found. But found or not, nobody will ever see me around these parts again! 50

SCENE 3

The senators are talking together when the soldier brings forth Antigone, tied up.

Sol.   Here's the woman who did it! We found her trying to bury him some more. Where's Creon?

Sen.   Here he comes out of the house.

(Creon enters.)

Cre.   What is it?

Sen.   My lord, I see a man should never vow he won't do something, because you can never tell what may happen. I could have sworn I'd never return after that burst of threats you rained down on me. But here I am, because now we've caught the woman who did the deed! No lot had to be cast this time; I wanted to be the one! So do what you think best; as for me, I'm through with the whole thing now.

Cre.   What are you talking about?   10

Sol.   We caught her burying the man herself!

Cre.   Are you serious?

Sol.   This girl tried to bury the body you said not to bury. Is that plain enough for you?

Cre.   How did you catch her?

Sol.   Like this. I went back and delivered your message. We swept off all the dust that had been put on the body and then went back a ways to keep an eye on it. Actually, we went back quite a ways, because the body was really putting out an aroma by this time! And we made sure to keep upwind of it. Well, people were trying to keep each other alert. About noon, when it was pretty hot, this whirlwind came along. It raised a cloud of dust all over the place, filling the air, and naturally we had to shut our eyes for a while. When the wind finally died down, we looked up, and here was this girl right there by the body! She called down curses on the people that had removed the coverings she had placed on the body earlier. Then she got handfuls of dust and poured drink-offerings on the body—three times. That was enough, and so we shot forward and grabbed her. She didn't deny anything, either the first time or the second. I felt sad and happy at the same time—sad for her but pleased as could be for myself!   25

Cre.   (to Antigone) Did you do this deed or not?

Ant.   I did; I deny nothing.

Cre.   (to Soldier) You may go. (Soldier leaves.) Tell me this, briefly: did you know about the order not to bury the body?

Ant.   Yes. How could I not know? It was plain enough.   30

Cre.   And you still broke the law?

Ant.   Yes, because it was your law, not that of the gods. The law doesn't fit with justice. I didn't think your law had enough power to override the unchangeable unwritten code of heaven, which didn't begin today or yesterday. It lives forever, and no one was around at its origin. I didn't want to provoke heaven by following the commands of a mortal. I knew I would die for this. Dying before my time I count as a plus. Surrounded by the sufferings my short life has had—why wouldn't I want to die? This isn't a bit painful to me. Now leaving my brother's body unburied—that would have been painful.

Sen.   When it comes to stubbornness, she's her father's child!   39

Cre.   But the stiffest piece gets broken first. If she wins this contest, then she's the man and I'm the woman! I don't care if she is my niece, I wouldn't care if she were my closest relative on earth—she and her sister, whom I suspect is equally involved with this, are doomed.

Ant.   Do you want anything else besides my life?

Cre.   No, just that.

Ant.   Then what are you waiting for? That's what it means to be a tyrant—the power to do whatever you like.

Cre. You're the only person who feels this way about the law.

Ant. No, lots of people in this town do; but they hold their tongues because of your threatened punishments.

Cre. Aren't you ashamed not to pay attention to what I said? 50

Ant. No, there's nothing shameful about honoring one's own flesh and blood.

Cre. Wasn't the man he killed your brother as well?

Ant. Yes.

Cre. Then aren't you insulting him by honoring his killer?

Ant. He's not the one protesting this.

Cre. But he died for his country, and his brother died against it.

Ant. Whoever dies deserves a decent burial.

Cre. Not equally decent for good and bad.

Ant. Are you sure that decent burial here isn't counted true religion there?

Cre. Even in death, an enemy is an enemy. 60

Ant. Well, I was made for fellowship and love, not for hate.

Cre. Then go down and love the dead. As long as I'm alive, no woman is going to order me around. (Ismene is brought in, guarded.) Ah, the other one. I've had the two of you staying in my palace, and you do this to me. Were you involved with this too, or are you innocent?

Isme. I am guilty too. That is, if Antigone says I am. I'm joining with her to share the blame.

Ant. No, you refused. I had no partner.

Isme. You're in trouble, so it's time for me to join in what you have to endure.

Ant. The dead spirits can tell who actually did the burying. A friend after the fact is no friend to me.

Isme. Don't shame me, sister, by denying me a death with you for honoring the dead. 70

Ant. But you didn't do it.

Isme. How could I live if you died this way?

Ant.   Ask Creon; you seem to think so much of him.

Isme.   **Why are you mocking me so, when it doesn't do any** good?

Ant.   If I'm mocking you, it's because I'm sick at heart.

Isme.   But the question is, what can I do to help you now?

Ant.   Save yourself.

Isme.   Don't I get to die with you?

Ant.   You chose to live, and I to die.

Cre.   One of these girls was born a fool, and the other has turned into one.   80

Isme.   How could I live without my sister?

Cre.   Don't say "my sister," because you don't have a sister any more.

Isme.   Would you kill your own son's fiancée?

Cre.   He can find other fields to plow.

Isme.   But they are promised to each other!

Cre.   I don't want unworthy wives for my sons.

Ant.   Dearest Haemon, your own father speaks badly of you.

Cre.   I'm tired of you and of hearing about your engagement.

Isme.   Your own son. Will you tear her from his arms?

Cre.   Death will do that for me.   90

Sen.   So you've decided on death, then?

Cre.   My mind is made up.

(Antigone and Ismene are led away.)

SCENE 4

Haemon comes to Creon and the senators.

Cre.   Son, are you here in anger, hearing the sentence against your fiancée? Or are we friends, always together, whatever our policies?

Hae.   I am yours, Father. You have guided my steps with good counsel, which I follow closely. No marriage is more important to me than the direction you have trained me to take, the path of honor.

Cre.   It is right for a son to support his father. This is why men pray for offspring—to have support in fighting their foes and in honoring their friends. Well done, my son; it is good not to fling away your wits through liking a woman; where a wife is evil, the bed is cold. What worse sore can pain us than a loved one's unworthiness? Better to spurn this maiden as a foe! Let her find a groom in the grave! She's the only one in the whole city who won't obey me. If I let my relatives break the rules, then you know strangers will. People must obey the laws of the state, big and small, just and unjust. A person who keeps laws can govern well and be governed well. You can trust that kind of comrade at your back in time of war. The biggest foe of any state is anarchy; a land lives by discipline. We're on the side of order around here. And if we had to lose, it would be better to be cast out by a man than by a woman.   15

Sen.   Unless I've grown senile, these are wise words.

Hae.   Father, the gods have given reason to mankind, the highest of all good gifts; and I'm reluctant to say you have spoken wrongly in anything. Still, another person's thoughts may be of service. And since I'm your son, it's up to me to notice what the people are doing and saying. The citizens are afraid to offend you because they're scared of you; but moving around quietly, I have discovered this: People feel sorry for Antigone. They say she was just trying to keep her brother from the hounds and the buzzards. They say, "She should have been carved in gold for this." Father, nothing is more important to me than your welfare; what can any decent son care more about than his father's honor? So I ask you not to think that whatever you say is always right and everyone else is wrong. Anyone who thinks he's the only person in a city with wisdom is empty. Even when a man is wise, he still needs to live and learn. We don't want to stick to a course too long. When trees bend with a winter wind, they survive; when they fight that wind, they break.

Father, cool down! Be willing to give in! My head is younger than yours, but it may still have some good sense. Admittedly, it would be best if everyone were born with perfect wisdom; but since that's not the way life is, we need to listen to wise counsel. 30

Sen. My lord, you might learn from him, when he speaks wisdom. And Haemon, you can learn from him. Both of you have spoken well.

Cre. Is it right for a man to learn from a boy?

Hae. Yes, when the boy is right. It's wrong to pay more attention to years than to wisdom.

Cre. You think it's wisdom to respect rebels?

Hae. I would never ask respect for a wrongdoer.

Cre. Don't you think she was a wrongdoer?

Hae. That's not what the people say.

Cre. Is the city supposed to tell me what laws to make?

Hae. There's no such thing as a one-man city. 40

Cre. So you're on the woman's side?

Hae. Only if you're a woman! I am for you.

Cre. You're trampling my paternal rights.

Hae. You're sinning against the right.

Cre. All this is for a woman.

Hae. And for you, and for me, and for the gods.

Cre. Whatever you say, she won't live long enough to marry you.

Hae. If she dies, she won't be the only one.

Cre. Is that a threat?

Hae. How is it a threat to try to counsel somebody? 50

Cre. You'll regret this "counseling."

Hae. If you weren't my father, I'd say you had gone crazy.

Cre. That remark will cost you dearly. Guards, bring out that woman at once, and let her die in front of him!

Hae.   Not in my sight! As for you, you don't even know who your friends are. You'll never see my face again. (He leaves.)

Sen.   My lord, a raging young man can be dangerous.

Cre.   It doesn't matter; he can't save those two girls.

Sen.   Both girls? Are you really planning to kill both of them?

Cre.   No, you're right; only the guilty one.   60

Sen.   How do you plan to kill her?

Cre.   She will be placed in a cave with enough food to survive, so that the city won't be guilty of her blood. Maybe buried alive she'll finally come to her senses.

SCENE 5

Antigone, guarded, is brought before Creon and the senate.

Cre.   Away with her! Wall her up in some deep vault, like I have said. Leave her there to die, if she wants. If she chooses to live, she can live in a tomb. We will be innocent of her blood, but she's not going to walk the earth any more.

Ant.   Father, Mother, Brother, I want your approval! I gain this fate from tending your body, Polynices. But to the wise it was no crime to honor you. If I have sinned, my suffering is just; but if the sin belongs to these who condemn me, may their punishment be measured by mine!

Cre.   If you guards let her keep talking, you're going to regret your slowness.

Ant.   (being led away) Thebes! My country! I die for a righteous cause!

SCENE 6

The blind prophet Tiresias is led by a boy to Creon and the senators.

Cre.	What do you want, honored Tiresias?
Tir.	I will tell you, but you need to obey.
Cre.	I have never parted from your advice.
Tir.	If you continue to listen to me, you'll steer the city well.
Cre.	I can testify that you've guided me wisely in the past.
Tir.	Then listen. You are walking on the razor's edge of disaster.
Cre.	What is it? You're making me tremble. 7

Tir.   When you hear what I have ascertained, you'll have reason to tremble. I just tried to give a burnt-offering to the gods, but the sacrifice wouldn't burn. Why? It's because the dead unhappy son of Oedipus has been left for dogs and birds, and now the gods won't accept our peace-offerings or sacrifices. Listen to me: everyone makes mistakes. But once a person makes a mistake, it's no mistake to turn around and go the opposite way. Continuing in a mistake is just plain stubbornness. Why do you want to try to punish the dead further? Where's the courage in that? I'm trying to give you good advice here, to help you out.

Cre.   I'm the target; everybody's shooting arrows at me, even soothsayers. But there's no way I'll permit that burial. And Tiresias, it's a shame when old men speak foul treason for the sake of getting paid off.

Tir.	Are you saying my oracles are false?
Cre.	I'm just saying prophets are greedy.
Tir.	And kings aren't? 20
Cre.	Do you know who you're talking to? I'm your lord.
Tir.	And you have helped protect our state; I'll give you that.
Cre.	And you're a wise man. But ….
Tir.	You're forcing me to say what I haven't told yet.

Cre.   Go ahead. Just make sure you haven't been paid by somebody to say it.

Tir.   Then listen to this: It's won't be much longer until you will make payment from your own house for what you've done, payment by death. You sent a living being, who didn't deserve it, to dwell in a tomb. Meanwhile you've kept a corpse out of the tomb! Fate will punish you for this, and quickly, too. Since you threw verbal wrath at me, I have paid you back. (to his guide) Boy, lead me back home again, so he can vent his spleen on younger men, and learn to keep a gentler tongue, and a wiser brain, than he carries now. (Tiresias and the guide leave.)   31

Sen.   The seer is gone, my lord, with his words of woe. And from the day my old hairs first began to turn from black to white, I have always known him as a watchdog who never barked in vain.

Cre.   I know it. It makes me uncomfortable—but it's so bitter to submit!

Sen.   Creon, you need wisdom right now!

Cre.   What should I do? Tell me; I'll listen.

Sen.   Go, set the maiden free from the vault, and build a tomb for that dead outcast.

Cre.   You're sure? You really think I should yield?

Sen.   Yes, I do, and with speed. Heaven sends calamities on people who are hard-hearted.

Cre.   But it's so hard! Well, I give up; I can't fight it any longer.   41

Sen.   Then get to work! Don't leave it for others to do!

Cre.   I'll start right now. Quickly, some of you men over there, get some axes up to that vault. I'll be there when you get there. I was the one who bound her, so I'll be the one to set her loose. I guess it's best to keep the old traditional laws all our lives.

SCENE 7

A messenger comes up to the senators.

Mess.   Citizens, no life stays the same, either good or bad. Fate raises people up and fate flings them back down, whether folks are generally happy or unhappy. There's no telling what will happen to us next. I thought Creon had a great life. He ruled this country, a flourishing country, and had absolute power; now, he's lost everything. He can hardly be even counted alive, now, for when a person has lost every single joy in life, he might as well be dead. He still has the power of a king, and he still has great riches at home; but if there's no delight at home, the rest is worthless. Power and wealth without joy are shadows.

Sen.   What new affliction to the royal family do you have to tell?

Mess.   Death is upon them—death caused by the living.

Sen.   Who is the slayer? And who is the victim?   10

Mess.   Haemon is no more. His life-blood is spilled, and by no stranger's hand.

Sen.   What! Was it his father, or himself?

Mess.   Self-slaughtered. He was furious with his father about the girl.

Sen.   O prophet! How quickly your words have come true! And now I see poor Eurydice, Creon's wife, coming toward us from the palace. It may be just chance, but perhaps she has heard her son's name.

Eury.   O all you citizens, I heard the sound of your speaking as I approached the gates, planning to bring my prayers to Athena. Just as I was getting ready to pray, a voice uttering woe to my household pierced my ears, and I shrank back in terror. But whatever the story is, tell it to me, for I am no novice; I can listen to misery.   20

Mess.   My dear mistress, I saw what happened, and will speak, and not vary from the truth in any way. Why should I soothe your ears with stories, only to be shown as a liar later? Truth is always right. I followed your husband to the plateau where the body of Polynices was still lying, though it had been partly eaten by dogs. We washed Polynices' body and then burned it on an altar of fresh-cut branches. We buried the remains and piled a monument of earth high over it all. Then, we went to the cell where Antigone was held, a chamber of death, a couch of stone. We were planning to break in, but when we got closer we saw the vault was already opened. Just then we heard this loud wail echo from the cave across the country. Creon heard it and started mumbling to himself, even as we continued in that direction. He said, "That was my son's voice. This may be the unhappiest path I will ever walk." To one of the guards he said, "Guard! Hurry down to that tomb and take a look. Tell me whether that was really the voice of Haemon, or whether my ears were deceiving me." I went with the guard to examine the tomb. We looked inside, and there we found Antigone, lying on the ground. She had hanged herself with a strip of linen. Haemon was down there with her, holding her around the waist, mourning his bride's death, and his father's deeds, and the wedding that would never be. Before we could report back, Creon came to the entrance and saw Haemon with Antigone. Creon started crying and said, "Antigone, what have you done? What was in your head? Why did you have to go so crazy?" Then he said to Haemon, "Son, come here, please. I'm begging you." Haemon just glared at him—never said a word. Then he walked over to his father, spit in his face, pulled his sword, and lunged for Creon's heart! But he missed. As soon as Creon saw the sword-thrust he dodged and ran. Mad at himself, Haemon jabbed the sword clear into the middle of his body. Still conscious, he clasped Antigone with his weakening arms, clinging to her. Gasping, he sprinkled her pale cheeks with great welling drops of blood. And now he lies there, dead, with his arms around the dead. His marriage is in and with the grave. His misery is a witness to humanity the woe that can come from a person not listening to wise counsel.   45

(Eurydice leaves.)

Sen.   What do you make of that? She went inside without saying a single word, either good or bad.

Mess.   That is strange. I hope that, hearing about this, she just doesn't want to make a public display of her mourning. Maybe she wants to go inside to do her crying privately. She understands self-control and decorum, and probably she just wants to do the right thing.

Sen.   Maybe so. But I get nervous when someone is too quiet.   51

Mess.   Perhaps you are right. I shall find out enter the house and see what is happening. You are right; the silence is ominous.

(The messenger leaves, and then Creon enters, carrying Haemon's body.)

Cre.   My dear son, you are dead for a fault of mine, no fault of your own!

Sen.   You have seen the truth, but too late.

Cre.   Yes, I have learned it and become wretched.

(The messenger enters.)

Mess.   O my master, now you must become even more wretched. You already have sorrows, and

I must bring you more.

Cre.   What more can there be?   59

Mess.   Your wife, the mother of the one you are holding, is dead, just now. You can see for yourself through the doors. (The palace doors are opened to show Eurydice's dead body by the altar.) She took a sharp dagger to her heart. In her last words she asked for evil to fall upon you and called you a child-slayer.

Cre.   Isn't there anyone here who will end my life with an iron blade? I don't want to live another day! (He goes into the palace, and the doors are shut.)

Sen.   The most important quality for a person to have, the foundation of life, is wisdom. Heaven will not allow a man to be irreverent. Those who make boastful, assertive speeches will find that heaven will rain down blows upon them, until, at last, men who live long enough come to find wisdom.

DR. FAUSTUS

◆

by Christopher Marlowe, c. 1590
(contemporized and abridged by Dr. Marv Hinten)

Introduction to Christopher Marlowe (1564–1593)

Christopher Marlowe died of a knife wound to the eye at the age of twenty-nine; clearly, his life was short but exciting.

It started more calmly, however. He was born in 1564 (the same year as Shakespeare) in Canterbury, England. His father was a shoemaker, which did not bode well for Marlowe's future education, but rich Elizabethans had set up scholarships for poor boys to go to secondary school and then college. Marlowe attended Cambridge University on one of these scholarships, under rather unusual circumstances. He took six years to complete his coursework, and at the end of that time (1587) the university decided not to grant him a degree because of excessive absences, much of it time spent on the continent of Europe. But Marlowe presented the university with a letter from Queen Elizabeth's royal council, indicating that Marlowe should get his degree because he "had done Her Majestie good service." Four hundred years later it's hard to know exactly what sort of service that was, but the vague phrasing suggests Marlowe may have been a spy.

So he received a Master's degree and set off for London. Marlowe's first play, *Tamburlaine*, about a Mongol conqueror, became an instant hit in London. People found both the plot and the style powerful. Marlowe produced about a play or two per year, becoming the first major playwright for the London stage. (The first permanent theaters in England had only been constructed about ten years earlier.) Marlowe wrote highly-regarded poetry that enhanced his reputation as well.

He managed, between plays, to get in and out of trouble, once being brought up on murder charges, another time on disturbing the peace. In fact, even the last week of his life the local government drew up a warrant for Marlowe's arrest, this time on charges of heresy and blasphemy. (It should be noted that the accuser, Marlowe's former roommate Thomas Kyd, was being tortured at the time and needed to accuse someone else to get himself off the hook.)

The warrant was not served on Marlowe, however, because he died first—and rather abruptly. On May 30, 1593, Marlowe spent a good bit of time drinking at a tavern with friends. They had an argument over (at least this is how the story goes) who should pay the bill, and Marlowe pulled out his dagger and wounded one of the men, Ingram Frizar. Frizar apparently grabbed the dagger and killed Marlowe with it, stabbing him just above the right eye. The London authorities, with their customary and admirable thoroughness, noted that the knife wound was two inches deep and one inch wide, and that the knife was worth twelve cents. Nothing was done to Frizar for the murder, which suggests that law enforcement officials may have felt the town of London now had one less troublemaker, and good riddance.

The original text of *Dr. Faustus* is—well, there is no such thing as an "original" text with this play. It exists in multiple versions and is perhaps the most corrupted manuscript of any Renaissance play. The play was written during a period when the English government urged (and in some cases required) playwrights to add political and religious (mainly anti-Catholic) propaganda to their dramas. This edition is greatly shortened from most, omitting all of the farcical portions (some of which may have been added by another author) and the propaganda.

CHARACTERS
Dr. Faustus
Mephistophilis, a demon
Lucifer, the highest demon
Good Angel
Bad Angel
Old Man
Friend (of Dr. Faustus)
Servant (of Dr. Faustus)
Chorus (an actor to make a closing commentary)
The Seven Deadly Sins

BACKGROUND: John Faustus has received his university degree and is trying to decide what area of specialization to give his life to.

SCENE 1

Faustus is alone in his study.

Fau.   Settle your studies, Faustus, and begin
To sound the depths of what you hope to teach.
Perhaps the field of logic should be mine.
But what does clever Aristotle say?
"To argue well is logic's greatest end."
Affords this art no greater miracle?
Then be a doctor, Faustus, heap up gold,
And be remembered for some wondrous cure.
"The goal of medicine is body's health."
Why, I have helped with plagues and maladies,   10
Yet am I still just Faustus and a man.
If I could make men live eternally,
Or, being dead, raise them to life again,
Then this profession were to be esteemed.
Goodbye to medicine. What about the law?
"If one thing and the same should be bequeathed
To party of the first part and as well
To party of the second part, one gets
The thing, the other gets the value of
The thing." Why, what a waste of time this is!   20
To be a lawyer is, I see, to be
A money-grubbing drudge. It's not for me.
When all is done, divinity* is best.
*[theology]
The Bible is the key, I'll study it.
"The wage of sin is death."* That's hard. "To say
*[Romans 6:23]
We have no sin is to deceive ourselves,

And then the truth is not in us."* So then, this means
*[I John 1:8. Significantly, Faustus does not read the next verse, which
says, "If we confess our sins, God is faithful and just to forgive us."]
We have to sin, and then we have to die—
To die an everlasting death. What kind
Of teaching's this? It's *Que, sera, sera*;   30
It's what will be, will be. Goodbye, religion!
Now these magicians' books are heavenly.
Lines, circles, scenes, letters, characters,
Yes, these are all the things that I desire.
Oh, what a world of profit and delight,
Of power, of honor, of omnipotence
Is promised to the studious artisan!
All things that move between the quiet poles
Shall be at my command. Emperors and kings
Are just obeyed within their separate states,   40
Nor can they raise the wind or shift the clouds;
But one whose domination rules in this
Can stretch as far as does the mind of man.
So I will try to raise a demon-servant up.

(Faustus picks up a book of spells, and Good Angel and Bad Angel
enter.)

G. An.   O Faustus! Lay that damned book aside;
Gaze not upon it lest it tempt your soul
And heap God's heavy wrath upon your head.
Go read the Scriptures; this is blasphemy.
B. An. Go forward, Faustus, in that famous art
Wherein all nature's treasure is contained;   50
You'll be on earth as Jove is in the sky,
Lord and Commander of the elements.

(Angels leave.)

Fau.   How am I swelling with ideas on this!
I'll make the spirits fetch me what I please
And answer every question that I have,
Perform whatever enterprise I want.
I'll have them fly to India for gold,
Ransack the ocean for the greatest pearl,
And search all corners of the new-found world
For pleasant fruits and princely delicacies.   60
I'll have them teach me in philosophy
And tell the secrets of all foreign kings.
It's night, so I'll begin to make my spells
And see if devils will obey my call. (He chants a spell.)

"Spirits of fire, air, water, hail!
Lucifer, Monarch of burning hell,
Make a powerful demon rise!"

(The demon Mephistophilis appears.)

Meph.   Now Faustus, what would you have me do?
Fau.   I charge you wait upon me while I live,
To do whatever deed I shall command,   70
Be it to make the moon drop from the sky
Or the ocean to overwhelm the world.
Meph.   I am a servant to great Lucifer
And may not follow thee without his leave.
No more than he commands can I perform.
Fau.   But I commanded you to come to me.
Meph.   The spell's the cause I came, but not by force;
For when we hear a person call us up,

We fly in hope to get his glorious soul.
Nor will we come, unless he use such means   80
Whereby he is in danger to be damned.
Therefore the shortest cut for conjuring's
To pray devoutly to the Prince of Hell.
Fau.   Which I have done.
To him I now do dedicate myself.
The word "damnation" terrifies me not.
So tell me, who's this Lucifer your lord?
Meph.   Arch-ruler and commander of all spirits.
Fau.   Was not that Lucifer an angel once?
Meph.   Yes, Faustus, and most dearly loved of God.   90
Fau.   How comes it then that he is prince of devils?
Meph.   O, by aspiring pride and insolence
For which God threw him from the face of heaven.
Fau.   And what are you that live with Lucifer?
Meph.   Unhappy spirits that fell with Lucifer,
Conspired against our God with Lucifer,
And are forever damned with Lucifer.
Fau.   Where are you damned?
Meph.   In hell.
Fau.   How happens it that you are out of hell?   100
Meph.   Why this is hell, nor am I out of it.
Think you that I who saw the face of God
And tasted the eternal joys of heaven
Am not tormented with ten thousand hells
In being deprived of everlasting bliss?
O Faustus! Leave these frivolous demands,
Which strike a terror to my fainting soul.
Fau.   What, is great Mephistophilis so passionate
For being deprived of the joys of heaven?
Now learn from me of manly fortitude   110

And scorn those joys you never will possess.
Now, bear these tidings to great Lucifer:
Since I have taken on eternal death,
Say I surrender up to him my soul,
If he will spare me four and twenty years,
Letting me live in all indulgence here,
Having you ever to attend on me,
To give me whatsoever I shall ask,
To tell me whatsoever I demand,
To slay my enemies and aid my friends,   120
And always be obedient to my will.
Go and return to mighty Lucifer.
Then meet me in my study at midnight
And there inform me what your master says.
Meph.   I will, Faustus.
Fau.   Had I as many souls as there are stars,
I'd give them all for Mephistophilis.

SCENE 2

Faustus is sitting in his study.

Fau.   Now I am fully damned, and can't be saved.
What use is it to think of God or heaven?
Away with such vain fancies, and despair:
Despair in God, and trust in Lucifer.
I can't go backward: no, I must be resolute.
Why am I wavering? O something's sounding in my ears:
"Give up this magic, turn to God again!"
Yes, and I will turn to God again.
To God? God loves me not.
The god I serve is my own selfish wants;   10

That's why I want the love of Lucifer.
To him I'll build an altar and a church.

(Good Angel and Bad Angel enter.)

G. An.   Sweet Faustus, leave that miserable art.
Fau.   Repentance, prayer, confession—will they work?
G. An.   O, they are means to bring you into heaven.
B. An.   They are illusions, fruits of fantasy,
That make men foolish who do trust them most.
G. An.   Sweet Faustus, think of heaven and heavenly things.
B. An.   No, Faustus, think of honor and of wealth.

(Angels leave.)

Fau.   Of wealth!   20
Why, I can have of anything I want.
When Mephistophilis shall stand by me,
What can God do to hurt me? I am safe.
I'll doubt no more. Come, Mephistophilis,
And bring glad tidings from great Lucifer.
Is it not midnight? Come, Mephistophilis! (Mephistophilis enters.)
Now tell me, what says Lucifer your lord?
Meph.   That I shall wait upon you while you live
If you will buy my service with your soul.
Fau.   Already I have promised you my soul.   30
Meph.   Faustus, you must bequeath it solemnly
And write a deed of gift with your own blood,
For that security craves great Lucifer.
If you deny it, I'll go back to hell.
Fau.   Wait, Mephistophilis, and tell me—what good
Will my soul do your lord?

Meph.	His kingdom.
Fau.	Is that the reason why he tempts us so?
Meph.	Misery loves company.
Fau.	Do you that torture others have pain, too? 40
Meph.	Our pain's as great as human souls do have.

But tell me, Faustus, shall I have your soul?
Then I will be your slave, and wait on you,
And give you more than you can think to ask.

Fau.   Yes, Mephistophilis, I'll give you it.

Meph.   Then, Faustus, stab your arm courageously
And bind your soul that at the proper day
Great Lucifer may claim it as his own;
Then you will be as great as Lucifer.

(Faustus stabs his arm.)

Fau.   Look, Mephistophilis, for love of you   50
I cut my arm, and with my very blood
Assure my soul to be great Lucifer's,
Chief lord and ruler of perpetual night.
See here the blood that trickles from my arm,
And let it work effect to make my wish.

Meph.   But, Faustus, you must
Write this in manner of a deed of gift.

Fau.   All right, I will. (He starts writing.) But Mephistophilis,
My blood congeals, and I can write no more.

Meph.   I'll fetch you fire to dissolve it quick.   60

(Mephistophilis leaves.)

Fau.   What might this clotting of my blood reveal?
Is it unwilling I should write this bill?

Why streams it not that I could finish up?
Faustus gives to you his soul. Right there it stopped.
Why couldn't I? Is not my soul my own?
I'll write it now: _Faustus gives to you his soul_.

(Mephistophilis comes back.)

Meph.   Here's fire. Come, Faustus, set it on.
Fau.   So now the blood begins to flow again,
And I will make an end immediately. (He writes.)
Meph.   (Aside) Oh, I'd do anything to get his soul!   70
Fau.   It is finished.* This bill is ended,
*[_The last words of Christ on the cross (John 19:30)_]
And here I have bequeathed my soul to Lucifer.
But what is this appearing on my arm?
Man, flee! Wherever should I flee?
If unto God, he'll throw me down to hell.
My senses are deceived; there's nothing here.
My arm is plain. I thought I saw the words,
Man, flee! But I will never flee.
Meph.   I'll fetch you something to delight your mind.

(Mephistophilis leaves and brings back some devils, who do a dance and leave.)

Fau.   Speak, Mephistophilis, what means this show?   80
Meph.   Nothing, Faustus, but to delight your mind
And show you now what magic can perform.
Fau.   But may I raise up spirits when I please?
Meph.   Yes, Faustus, and do greater things than these.
Fau.   Then that's enough to give a thousand souls.
Here, Mephistophilis, receive this scroll,

A deed of gift of body and of soul,
Upon condition, though, that you perform,
All articles prescribed between us both.
Meph.   Faustus, I swear by hell and Lucifer   90
To keep all promises between us made.
Fau.   Then hear me read them:
I, John Faustus, with a doctorate from
Wittenburg University, do hereby give
both body and soul to Lucifer, Prince
of Hell, and his assistant Mephistophilis;
I furthermore grant to them, after the
expiration of twenty-four years, assuming
the articles below are kept, full power to
fetch my body, soul, and goods into their   100
habitation, wherever that may be. This
grant is made upon the following conditions:
First, that Faustus may be a spirit in form
and substance.
Secondly, that Mephistophilis shall be
Faustus' servant, at his command.
Thirdly, that Mephistophilis shall bring
to Faustus whatever he desires and do
anything for him.
Fourthly, that Mephistophilis shall remain   110
invisible to others in Faustus' house.
Lastly, that Mephistophilis shall appear
to Faustus at any time requested, in
whatever shape or form is requested.
By me, John Faustus.
Meph.   Speak, Faustus, do you deliver this as your deed?
Fau.   Yes, take it, and the devil make it good.
Meph.   Now, Faustus, ask whatever you want.

Fau.   First I will question you about hell.
Tell me, where is the place that men call hell?   120
Meph.   Under heaven.
Fau.   Yes, but where?
Meph.   Within the midst of these elements,
Where we are tortured and remain forever.
Hell has no limits, nor is it bound up
Into one clear place; for where we are is hell,
And where hell is there must we ever be.
And to conclude, when all the world dissolves,
And every creature shall be purified,
All places shall be hell that are not heaven.   130
Fau.   Come, I think hell's a fable.
Meph.   Yes, think so still, till experience changes your mind.
Fau.   So, do you think then that I will be damned?
Meph.   Yes, necessarily, for here's the scroll
Wherein you've given your soul to Lucifer.
Fau.   Yes, and body too—but what of that?
Think you that I'm so stupid as to think
That, after this life, there is any pain?
Tut, these are fables, and mere old wives' tales.
Meph.   But Faustus, I am an instance to prove the contrary,   40
For I am damned and am now in hell.
Fau.   What! Now in hell?
Why, if this is hell, I'll willingly be damned here.
What, walking, talking, etc.?
But, moving on now, let me have a wife,
The fairest maid in Germany,
For I have wants and lusts
And cannot live without a wife.
Meph.   What—a wife!
I beg you, Faustus, talk not of a wife.   150

Fau.   Sweet Mephistophilis, fetch me one,
For I will have one.
Meph.   Well—you will have one. Sit there till I come.
I'll fetch you a wife, in the devil's name.

(Mephistophilis leaves and comes back bringing a demon dressed like a woman, with fireworks.)

Meph.   Tell me, Faustus, how do you like your wife?
Fau.   She's nothing but a hot whore!
Meph.   Faustus, marriage is just a ceremony.
If you love me, think no more of it.
I'll cull you out some gorgeous prostitutes
And bring them every morning to your bed.   160
Whomever your eye likes, your heart will have.
(He hands Faustus a book of spells.)
Here, take this book to study thoroughly.
Call whirlwinds, tempests, thunder and lightning,
And men in armor shall appear to you,
Ready to execute what you desire.
Fau.   Thanks, Mephistophilis. But I
Would like a book wherein I might behold
Spells and incantations to bring up spirits
When I please.
Meph.   (handing another book) Here they are, in this book.   170
Fau.   Are you sure this will work?
Meph.   I promise.

SCENE 3
Faustus is talking with Mephistophilis.

Fau.   When I behold the heavens, then I repent,
And curse you, wicked Mephistophilis,

Because you have deprived me of those joys.
Meph.   Why, Faustus, do you think
Heaven's such a glorious thing?
I tell you it's not half as fair as you
Or any man who breathes upon the earth.
Fau.   How do you figure that?
Meph.   It was made for people;
Therefore people are more excellent.   10
Fau.   If it was made for people, it was made for me;
I will renounce this magic and repent.

(Good Angel and Bad Angel enter.)

G. An.   Faustus, repent; God will still pity you.
B. An.   You're now a spirit*; God can't pity you.
*[*In point 1 of the contract, Faustus asked to be a spirit rather than a
human.*]
Fau.   Who buzzes in my ear that I'm a spirit?
If I'm a devil, yet God may pity me.
Yes, God will pity me if I repent.
B. An.   Yes, but Faustus never will repent.

(Angels leave.)

Fau.   My heart's so hardened I cannot repent.
Scarce can I name salvation, faith, or heaven,   20
But fearful echoes thunder in my ears,
Faustus, you are damned!" Then swords and knives,
Poison, guns, nooses, and envenomed steel
Are laid before my to dispatch myself.
And long ere this I would have slain myself
Had not sweet pleasure conquered deep despair.

I am resolved; I never shall repent.
Come, Mephistophilis, and let's discuss
Astronomy. Tell me, who made the world?
| Meph. | I will not. | 30 |

Fau.   Sweet Mephistophilis, tell me.
Meph.   Urge me not, for I won't tell you.
Fau.   Villain, have I not bound you to tell me anything?
Meph.   Yes, anything not against our kingdom; but this is.
Fau.   I need to think about God who made the world.
Meph.   Think instead on hell, Faustus, because you are damned.
Fau.   Go, accursed spirit, to ugly hell.
It's you who has damned my distressed soul.
(Mephistophilis leaves.) Is it too late?

(Good and Bad Angels return.)

| B. An. | Too late. | 40 |

G. An.   Never too late, if you can repent.
B. An.   If you repent, devils will tear you to pieces.

(Angels leave, and Mephistophilis returns with Lucifer.)

Luc.   Christ cannot save your soul, for he is just;
No one but I have interest in your soul
Fau.   Who are you?
Luc.   I am Lucifer.
Fau.   Oh no! Have you come to fetch away my soul?
Luc.   I've come to tell you that you injure me.
You think of God, contrary to your promise.
You should not think of God; think of me, instead.   50
Fau.   I won't mistake again. Pardon me in this,
And I promise never to look to heaven,

Never to name God, or to pray to him.
Luc.   Do so, and we'll take care of you.
Faustus, I've come from hell to entertain you.
Sit down, and you'll see the Seven Deadly Sins.
Fau.   That will be a pleasing sight.

(The Seven Deadly Sins enter.)

Fau.   Who are you—the first one?
Pri.   I am Pride. I can do anything.
I can—Say, it stinks in here!   60
I'm not going to say another word,
Unless you perfume the ground and
Cover it with a lovely tapestry.
Fau.   Who are you—the second?
Gre.   I am Greed. If I had my wish,
Everything in this house, including you,
Would be turned into gold.
Fau.   Who are you—the third?
Ang.   I am Anger. If I don't have anybody
Else to fight with, I can get mad at myself.   70
Fau.   Who are you—the fourth?
Env.   I am Envy. I can't read, so I wish
All the books in the world were burnt. Say,
What's this—you're sitting down and I'm
Standing! Give me that chair!
Fau.   Go away, you rascal! Who are you—the fifth?
Glut.   Me, sir? I am Gluttony. I'm a little
Weak right now—squeaking by on 30 meals a
Day. Say, Faustus, will you invite me to supper?
Fau.   No, you'd eat too much. Who are you—the sixth?   80
Slo.   I am Sloth. I spend every day lying

On a sunny bank. What'd you make me leave
For, anyway? I'm too tired to say another word.
Fau. And you, Lady, last in line, who are you?
Lus. I, sir? I am Lust, and I always say an
Ounce of aphrodisiacs is worth a pound of impotence.
Luc. Back to hell, all of you. (The Sins leave.)
Now, Faustus, how do you like this?
Fau. This is great!
Luc. Faustus, in hell we have all manner   90
Of delight like this.
Fau. I wish I could see hell and come back again.
That would really make me happy!
Luc. You will; I'll come for you at midnight.
Farewell, Faustus, and remember to think of me.
Fau. Farewell, great Lucifer!

SCENE 4

Faustus' servant is in the living room of Faustus' house.

Serv. I think my master expects to die shortly,
For he has given me all his goods;
And yet, I think, if death were near,
He would not feast tonight with a friend.
The meal is over; here they come.

(Faustus enters with a friend. Mephistophilis also enters, invisible.)

Frie. Faustus, I've heard that Helen of Troy
Was supposed to be the most beautiful
Woman who ever lived. If you wouldn't

Mind doing me the favor of showing me
What she looked like, I would really appreciate it.   10
Fau.   Sir, you shall behold that peerless
Lady of Greece, just the way she was
When Paris took her.

(There is music, and Helen walks across the stage.)

Frie.   No marvel though the angry Greeks pursued
With ten years' war the rape of such a queen,
Whose heavenly beauty passes all compare.
I will depart; but for this glorious deed
Happy and blessed be Faustus evermore.
Fau.   Sir, farewell; the same I wish to you.

(The friend and the servant leave; an old man enters.)

Old.   Ah, Doctor Faustus, I want to prevail
To guide your steps into the way of life.
Ask mercy, Faustus, of your Savior sweet,
Whose blood alone can wash away your guilt.
Fau.   What have I done?
I'm damned, damned; I might as well die!

(Mephistophilis hands him a dagger.)

Old.   O wait, good Faustus, hold your desperate hand!
I see an angel hovering over your head,
Who with a vial full of precious grace,
Is ready to pour it all into your soul.
So call for mercy and avoid despair.   30
Fau.   Ah, my sweet friend, I feel

Your words do comfort my distressed soul.
Leave me a while to ponder on my sins.
Old.   I go, sweet Faustus, but with heavy heart,
Fearing the ruin of your hopeless soul. (He leaves.)
Fau.   Accursed Faustus, where is mercy now?
I do repent; and yet I do despair.
Hell strives with grace for conquest in my heart.
What shall I do to shun the snares of death?
Meph.   You traitor, Faustus, I arrest your soul   40
For disobedience to my sovereign lord;
Return, or I'll in pieces tear your flesh.
Fau.   Sweet Mephistophilis, beg your lord
To pardon my unjust behavior,
And with my blood again I will confirm
My former vow I made to Lucifer.
Meph.   Do it then quickly, with sincere heart,
Lest danger do attend your drift. (Faustus does.)
Fau.   Torment, sweet friend, that base old man,
Who dared persuade me from my Lucifer,   50
With greatest torments that our hell affords.
Meph.   His faith is great, I cannot touch his soul;
But what I may afflict his body with
I will attempt, which isn't worth much.
Fau.   One thing, good servant, let me ask of you:
That I might have as my lover
That heavenly Helen, whom I just saw,
Whose sweet embracing may extinguish clean
The thoughts that do persuade me from my vow,
So I can keep the oath I made to Lucifer.   60
Meph.   Faustus, this and all else you desire
Shall be performed in the twinkling of an eye.

(Helen comes back in.)

Fau.   Was this the face that launched a thousand ships?
Sweet Helen, make me immortal with a kiss! (They kiss.)
Here will I dwell, for heaven is in these lips,
And all is trash that is not Helen.

SCENE 5

Faustus and his friend are talking; it is the day the 24 years are up.

Fau.   Oh, sir!
Frie.   What ails you, Faustus?
Fau.   Deadly sin that has damned me.
Frie.   Faustus, look to heaven; God's mercies are infinite.
Fau.   Not for this. To gain the powers I have—I gave my soul
to Lucifer.
Frie.   God forbid!
Fau.   God did forbid it, but I did it anyway.
For 24 years of pleasure I gave up eternal joy.
The time is expired, midnight will come,
And he will fetch me.   10
Frie.   Why didn't you tell me of this
Before, so I could pray for you?
Fau.   I often thought about doing so,
But the Devil threatened to tear me in pieces
If I named God; and now it is too late.
You'd better leave, lest you perish with me.
Frie.   What can I do to save you?
Fau.   Nothing. Just leave and save yourself.
Whatever noise you hear, do not come in,

For nothing can rescue me.   20
Frie.   But pray, and I will pray that God
May have mercy upon you.
Fau.   Farewell! If I live till morning,
I'll visit you; if not—I have gone to hell.

(The friend leaves, and the clock strikes eleven.)

Fau.   Ah, Faustus,
Now you have but one bare hour to live,
And then you must be damned perpetually!
Stand still, you ever-moving spheres of heaven,
That time may cease and midnight never come.
Fair nature's sun, rise, rise again and make   30
Perpetual day; or let this hour be but
A year, a month, a week, a normal day,
So that I can repent and save my soul.
The stars move still. Time runs, the clock will strike,
The devil will come, and I will be damned.
O, I'll leap up to my God! Who pulls me down?
See, see where Christ's blood streams in the heavens!
One drop would save my soul—
half a drop. Ah, my Christ!
It tears my heart to name the name of Christ.   40
Yet will I call on him: O spare me, Lucifer!
Where is it now? It's gone, and see where God
Stretches out his arm and bends his angry brows.
Mountains and hills come, come and fall on me,
And hide me from the heavy wrath of God!

(The clock strikes 11:30.)

Ah, half the hour is past! It will all be past soon!
Oh, God!
If you will not have mercy on my soul,
Yet for Christ's sake whose blood has ransomed me,
Impose some end to my incessant pain;   50
Let me live in hell a thousand years—
A hundred thousand, and at last be saved!
O, no end is limited to damned souls.
Why wasn't I a creature lacking soul?
The beasts are happy, for when they die,
Their souls are soon dissolved in elements,
But mine must live, ever to be plagued in hell.
Cursed be the parents that engendered me!
No. I must curse myself, curse Lucifer,
That have deprived me of the joys of heaven.   60

(The clock strikes 12:00.)

O, it strikes, it strikes! Now, body, turn to air,
Or Lucifer will bear you straight to hell.

(Thunder and lightning.)

O soul, be changed into little water-drops
And fall into the ocean, never to be found.
My God! My God! Look not so fierce on me!

(Devils enter.)

Adders and serpents, let me breathe awhile!
Ugly hell, gape not! Come not, Lucifer!
I'll burn my books! Ah, Mephistophilis!

(The devils leave with Faustus, and the chorus-actor
comes in for the closing commentary.)

Cho.   Cut is the branch that might have grown full straight,
That used to grow within this learned man.   70
Faustus is gone; regard his hellish fall,
Whose evil fortunes may exhort the wise.

PARABLE OF THE CAVE

◆

Told by Socrates, written by Plato, c. 400 B.C.

(Translated by Benjamin Jowett, contemporized and abridged
by Dr. Marv Hinten)

INTRODUCTION TO SOCRATES (470–399 B.C.) AND PLATO (428–347 B.C.)

Socrates, like Jesus and Confucius, did not write down his thoughts for posterity; our knowledge of his ideas comes (again as with the other two teachers) from disciples. The primary disciple of Socrates that we know today was Plato, about 40 years younger than his teacher. If you sometimes see works such as "Parable of the Cave" attributed to Socrates, and sometimes to Plato, this is the reason; Socrates told the parable, Plato wrote it down.

Socrates lived in what is often called the "Golden Age" of ancient Athens, at about the same time as the playwright Sophocles. Socrates determined early in life to devote himself to trying to answer this question: What is the best way to live? The first piece here is a parable (a story with a higher meaning) speculating on what would be the fate of a person who did come to believe in a far nobler way of life and try to live by it. Socrates felt this person would be misunderstood and considered dangerous. His life, and the life of Jesus (another famous parable-maker), show that this speculation is probably accurate.

According to legend, the oracle at Delphi said that Socrates was the wisest man in Athens. He found this hard to believe, so he went around asking questions of others (the "Socratic method") to see how much wisdom they had. To his surprise, other people always seemed to pretend to more knowledge than they really had; they found it hard to admit ignorance. Socrates therefore reasoned that perhaps the oracle was right, for he remained constantly aware of how little he knew about life, logic, and religion.

Socrates taught his followers to continually reach for more knowledge, primarily by asking their elders, "How do you know this is right?" He caused them to question everything that their parents and leaders did, and needless to say, the leaders didn't like it. Therefore, near the end of his long life, Socrates was brought to trial on a charge of "corrupting the youth." Of the 500 voters (standard for a trial in ancient Athens), 270 voted him guilty. The prosecutor then called for the death penalty. Rather than asking for exile, as expected, Socrates indicated Athens should actually express financial appreciation for his way of life! But he said he would be willing to pay a negligible fine. Outraged by this cavalier attitude, the citizens voted Socrates the death penalty.

The second piece here, about Socrates' death, shows how calmly he accepted his fate. One point that this piece does not mention: After his sentencing, Socrates was given the opportunity to escape. He chose instead to accept the punishment determined by the state, feeling that that was part of being a good citizen.

PARABLE OF THE CAVE

NOTE: Socrates is telling this dialogue to a man named Glaucon. For clarity, I have put Socrates' words in regular type and Glaucon's responses in italics.

And now, let me show in a figure of speech how far our nature is enlightened or unenlightened. Behold some human beings living in an underground den, which has a mouth open toward the light and reaching all along the den. Here they have been from their childhood, and have their legs and necks chained so that they cannot move, and can only see in front of them, being prevented by the chains from turning around their heads. Above and behind them a fire is blazing at a distance, and between the fire and the prisoners there is a raised way. And you will see, if you look, a low wall built along the way, like the screen which puppet players have in front of them to cover their bodies, over which they show the puppets.

I see.

And you can see people passing along the wall carrying all sorts of vessels, and statues, and figures of animals made of various materials, which appear over the wall. Some of them are talking, others silent.

You have shown me a strange image, and they are strange prisoners.

They are like us. Now, they see only shadows, which the fire throws on the opposite wall of the cave, correct?

True. How could they see anything but the shadows if they were never allowed to move their heads?

And similarly, of the objects which are being carried they would only see the shadows?

Yes.

And if they were able to talk with each other, wouldn't they suppose that they were naming what was actually in front of them?

Very true.

And suppose further that the prison had an echo which came from the other side, wouldn't they imagine when one of the passers-by spoke that the voice came from the shadow?

Unquestionably.

To them, the shadows would be literally the truth.

That is certain.

Now look again, and see what will happen if one of the prisoners is released and discovers his error. At first, when this man is liberated, stands up, and walks toward the light, he will suffer pains; the glare will distress him, and he will be unable to see the realities. Now imagine him outside, and someone saying to him that what he saw before was an illusion, but that now, when his eye is seeing reality, he has a clearer vision. What will be his reply? And you may further imagine his instructor pointing to objects as they pass and asking him to name them. Won't he be perplexed? Won't he at first think the shadows he used to see are truer then the objects now being shown to him?

Yes.

If this man is out in bright sunlight, isn't he likely to be physically irritated?

Yes, for a while.

He will need time to grow accustomed to the sight of the upper world. First he will see shadows best, then reflections, then the objects themselves. And won't he see the sky and stars by night better than the sunlight by day?

Certainly.

Last of all would he be able to see the sun.

Definitely.

Finally he would be able to reason that this is what gives seasons and years, what makes the world visible.

Yes, when he can finally see the sun he will reason this out.

Then when he remembers his old dwelling-place, don't you think he will believe he is wiser now, and feel sorry for the people in the den?

Certainly.

Suppose they were in the habit of conferring honors among themselves on those who were quickest to identify the passing shadows. Do you think he would care about honors and awards like that any more?

No, he would consider that silly.

Now, imagine this man coming down out of the sunlight to be placed again in his old situation. Wouldn't his eyes once again be full of darkness?

Yes.

And imagine there were a contest, and he had to compete in recognizing the shadows with the prisoners who had never moved out of the den, while his eyes are still used to the light; wouldn't he seem ridiculous? The cavedwellers would say of him that he returned without his eyesight, and it is better not to go outside the cave. And if anyone tried to take another person outside the cave, if they could catch the offender, it would be best to put him to death.

Indeed.

This entire parable you may interpret this way: The prison-cave is the world of sight, the light of the fire is the sun, and the journey out of the cave is the ascent of the soul into a higher understanding. I have expressed this according to my belief—whether rightly or wrongly, God knows. But whether this is true or false, my opinion is that in our world the idea of true good appears last of all, and is seen only with an effort. When it is seen, people can reason out that this true good is the author of all things right and beautiful, the source of reason and truth in the intellectual realm; to act rationally, whether publicly or privately, a person needs to keep his mind's eye on this power of good.

I agree, as far as I am able to understand you.

Now, if any people do attain the ability to see this power of highest good, it's no wonder if regular human affairs lose interest for them; for these people want to live in the higher world—which is understandable, if our allegory can be trusted.

Yes, it's very natural.

Therefore, anyone with common sense will recognize that inability to see naturally can be of two types, and arise from two different causes: either from coming into the light, or going out of the light. This is as true of the mental/spiritual eye as of the physical eye. A person who keeps this in mind when he sees a person looking at things differently will not be too quick to laugh. He will ask first why it is that this person can't see by our natural level of light: Has this person has come out of a brighter life, now not seeing "normally" because he is unused to darkness, or does this person simply have a darkened mind that can't see by natural light? The first person is to be admired, the second to be pitied.

That is a very wise distinction.

DEATH OF SOCRATES

◆

by Plato, c. 399 B.C.
(Translated by Benjamin Jowett, contemporized and abridged by
Dr. Marv Hinten)

NOTE: This conversation occurs on the last day of Socrates' life, with
Plato and a few other close friends around, while Socrates is awaiting
the hemlock (poison) for his death penalty.

"Let a man be of good cheer about his soul," Socrates said, "who has
adorned the soul with its own proper jewels: temperance, justice,
courage, nobility, and truth. Dressed in these, the soul is ready to go on
its next journey when the time comes. All of you here will depart at
some time or other. I am being called by the voice of fate already. Soon
I must drink the poison; so I think I had better go bathe first, so the
women won't have the trouble of washing my body after I am dead."

When he had finished, Crito said, "Do you have any commands for
us, Socrates—anything to say about your children, or any other matter
in which we can serve you?"

"Nothing in particular," Socrates replied. "Only, as I have always said,
I would like you to take care of yourselves; that would be a service to me

as well as to you. And you don't need to make a vow or oath about it; if you haven't been taking care of yourselves already, making an oath won't do any good at this point."

"We will do our best," Crito said. "But how do you want us to bury you?"

"However you like—just get hold of me and don't let me get away!" Socrates smiled and turned to the rest of us, saying, "I can't make Crito believe that I am the same Socrates who has always been here. He's already thinking of me as that other Socrates whom he'll see soon, the dead body; so he wants to know how to bury me. Even though I have said repeatedly that when I have drunk the poison I will enter the joy of the blessed, these words of mine, which have comforted me and the rest of you, have had no effect on Crito. Therefore I want the rest of you to pledge a bond for him, just as he pledged a bond for me at the trial— but let it be a bond of a different sort. Crito pledged a bond for me at the trial to the judges that I would remain, but I want you to promise Crito that I will not remain, but will depart; then he will suffer less at my death and not be grieved when he sees my body being buried or burned. I don't want him saying at the grave, 'Now we are burying Socrates.' False words are not only evil in themselves, but they infect the soul with evil. Be of good cheer, then, my dear Crito, and say that you are burying only my body, and with that you can do whatever is usual, as you think best."

When he had spoken these words, he rose and went into the bath chamber, asking us to wait. We waited, talking and thinking of the greatness of our sorrow. He was like a father that we were going to lose, leaving us to spend the rest of our lives as orphans. After he had taken the bath his children were brought to him (he had two young sons and one older one), and the women of his family came also. He gave them a few directions, talked with them a bit, and then dismissed them and returned to us.

It was now almost sunset, for a good bit of time had passed while he was gone. When he came back after his bath, he sat with us again, but not much was said. After a bit the jailer came in and said, "Socrates, you are the noblest and gentlest and best person ever confined in this place. Other men rage and swear at me when I tell them to obey the authorities and drink the poison. But I am sure you won't be angry with me, since you are aware I am not the person deciding this. So best wishes, and try to bear lightly what is coming; you know what I have to do." Then bursting into tears, he turned and went out.

As he left, Socrates said, "I return your good wishes and will do what you tell me." Turning to us, Socrates remarked, "What a kind man he is! My whole time here in prison he has talked with me and been as good as he could be; and now you see how generously he sorrows for me. Well, we must do what he says. If the poison is ready, let the cup be brought; if not, let it be prepared."

Crito said, "The sun is still on the hilltops, and lots of times people drink the poison late, well after the announcement has been made; sometimes they even take a meal. So don't hurry; there's still time left."

Socrates answered, "Crito, the people you are talking about are right to delay, because they think they're better off here. But I am right not to delay, for I don't see myself gaining anything by drinking the poison a little bit later. It would be trying to save a life that is already gone; I would laugh at myself for doing so. Please do as I have said."

When Crito heard this, he made a sign to the servant, who went to fetch the jailer with the poison. Socrates said to the jailer, "My good friend, you are experienced in these matters, so tell me how to go about this."

The jailer answered, "After drinking, just walk around until your legs feel heavy, then lie down, and the poison will act."

He handed the cup to Socrates, who didn't act the least bit scared or nervous. Taking the cup, Socrates asked, "May I pour a bit of this in consecration as an offering to a god?"

The jailer replied, "Socrates, we only prepare just as much as we think necessary."

"I understand," Socrates said. "But I must pray to the gods to prosper my journey from this world to the other one. This now is my prayer, and may it be granted to me."

Then lifting the cup to his lips, quite readily and cheerfully he drank up the poison.

Up to this point most of us had been able to control ourselves. But now when we saw him drinking, and saw that he drank the whole thing, we couldn't hold off any longer. I tried, but I couldn't help it; tears were just pouring out of me. Yet it wasn't for him; I was crying for myself at having lost such a wonderful friend.

I wasn't the only one. Crito was crying so hard he moved across the room; I did the same; then Apollodorus, who'd been sobbing the whole time, started crying so hard it made cowards out of all of us. Socrates was the only man there who wasn't crying. "What's this strange outburst?" he asked. "I sent the women out of the room to avoid this sort of thing, because I have always believed a man should die peacefully. Be quiet, and have patience."

When we heard that, we were ashamed, and calmed ourselves down. He walked around until he said his legs were having trouble moving. Then he lay down on his back, according to the directions, and the jailer now and then examined his feet and legs. After a while the jailer pressed Socrates' foot hard and asked if he could feel that. Socrates said he couldn't. The jailer moved up the legs and showed us they were cold and stiff.

Socrates felt his legs himself and said, "When the poison reaches the heart, that will be the end." When he was beginning to grow cold about the groin, he uncovered his face (which he had covered himself) and said his last words: "Crito, I owe a rooster to Asclepius;* will you

*[Since Asclepius was the Greek god of healing, most commentators think Socrates is wanting a thank-offering made for his peaceful transition to a better world.]

remember to pay the debt?"

"The debt will be paid," Crito replied. "Is there anything else?" No answer came to this question. A moment or two later we noticed Socrates' eyes were fixed, and Crito closed his eyes and mouth.

This was the end of our friend, who I may truly call the wisest, noblest, best man I have ever known.

ANALECTS

◆

by Confucius (c. 500 B.C.)
(Translated by William Soothill, contemporized and abridged
by Dr. Marv Hinten)

INTRODUCTION TO CONFUCIUS
(551–479 B.C.)

Most Western readers know very little about Confucius, associating him with fortune cookies and standard proverbs (preceded by the phrase "Confucius say"). But he is the most influential thinker in the history of China.

Confucius' father was a soldier and governor of a small area; the family was what we might consider upper middle-class. Confucius married at nineteen and shortly thereafter took a minor political office; but his main interest in life was always knowledge, and sometime during the next few years he became a public teacher and acquired some disciples. As he became more famous, he visited various parts of China, attempting to provide guidance to rulers of provinces. Most of ancient China had as little enthusiasm for wisdom as most of contemporary America, so Confucius' efforts were not appreciated. He spent the last twenty years of his life in a meandering search to find a ruler who would set up a state guided by enlightenment, but the venture failed.

After Confucius died, his followers began compiling his oral teachings, and these were eventually collected as the *Analects (Sayings)*. They probably did not reach their final form until about 400 B.C.

NOTE: Most of the sayings begin with some form of "The Master said." I have eliminated that phrase to avoid repetitiousness. Numbering of the sayings sometimes varies slightly in some translations.

ANALECTS

19.19 If you govern people by laws and penalties, they will learn to avoid the penalties but will not have a sense of shame. If you govern them by moral excellence and role modeling, they will live by those standards and feel ashamed when they do not.

19.20 For most people nowadays, taking care of parents means making sure they have enough to live on; but we do that even for dogs and horses. Unless honor is added in, what's the difference between parents and animals?

19.21 What does it take to be a teacher? Keep reviewing old knowledge and keep acquiring new knowledge.

19.22 Don't worry about not having a high position; instead be concerned about becoming worthy of a high position.

19.23 Most people know only what something costs; wise people know whether something is good.

19.24 Jan Chiu said, "I appreciate your teachings, Sir, but I don't have strength enough to carry them out." Confucius said, "A person who isn't strong enough gives out part-way through the task, but you say it's too hard before you try."

19.25 What can upset me? Neglect in improving my character, lack of thoroughness in study, failing to do my duty, inability to correct my imperfections.

19.26 I only explain things to a person who really wants to know. If I demonstrate one angle of a rectangle to someone, and they don't bring me back the other three, then I don't bother teaching them any more.

19.27 Tzu Lu said, "If you were in charge of an army, who would you want with you? Confucius said, "I wouldn't want a man who is ready to take on a tiger with his bare hands. I want a man who loves strategy and success and has a suitable fear of losing."

19.28 Tzu Lu had been asked what kind of person Confucius was. Confucius said, "Here's what you should have answered: 'Confucius is a man so eager for improvement he sometimes forgets to eat, so happy that he sometimes forgets his sorrows, a man who doesn't worry about getting older.'"

19.29 Tzu Kung asked, "If somebody gives me a valuable gem, should I keep it locked away somewhere or should I sell it?" "Sell it! Sell it!" responded Confucius. Then he added, "But wait till you get a good offer."

19.30 Some people study but don't advance toward truth; some people advance toward truth but don't take a firm stand; some people take a firm stand but don't use good judgment.

19.31 Do not do to others what you would not want them to do to you.

19.32 The essentials of effective government, in order of importance, are the confidence of the people, sufficient food, and sufficient armed forces.

19.33 I can try a lawsuit as well as anyone else, but it's a greater thing to keep lawsuits from coming about in the first place.

19.34 If you hear of a certain person that "Everybody likes him" or "Nobody likes him," that doesn't mean much. What's important is that the good people like him and the bad people don't.

19.35 If a person has 300 pages of textbooks practically memorized but can't figure out how to handle a new situation, what good did those textbook pages do?

19.36Can you care about someone under you without making them work hard? Can you do your best for someone without trying to educate them?

19.37If a person could learn from your words, and you don't bother to talk with them, you're wasting that person. If you're trying to teach someone who isn't a learner, you're wasting your words. It's wise not to waste words or people.

19.38If you're strict with yourself but understanding with others, you'll avoid a lot of ill will.

19.39Human nature is fairly consistent. People diverge from one another by what they habitually practice.

19.40Wise people seem different, depending on how well you know them. From afar they can appear stern. If you approach them, they seem gracious. If you converse with them, you notice their clear thinking.

THE KORAN

◆

By Muhammed, c. 610

(Translated by George Sale, contemporized and abridged by Dr. Marv Hinten)

INTRODUCTION TO MUHAMMED (c. 570–632)

Muhammed, founder of Islam (Arabic for "surrender"), was born in Mecca, Saudi Arabia, around 570. His childhood was a series of losses; in fact, his father died before Muhammed was born. At the age of six, when Muhammed lost his mother, he was sent to live with his grandfather; but the grandfather died when Muhammed was eight. He then moved in with an uncle, a tribal head who engaged in trading. Despite all the moving around, Muhammed seems to have had a relatively well-adjusted childhood.

In his twenties he worked for a wealthy widow named Khadijah, and, impressed with his character and business skills, she asked for his hand in marriage. He agreed, despite the difference in their ages (she was late 30s, he was middle 20s) and the large number of children she already had (seven). The marriage seemed to be both happy and prolific; they produced six more children as a couple. Muhammed did not practice polygamy, incidentally, until after Khadijah's death.

Muhammed was always a religious man and would occasionally leave town for a quiet night of meditation. During one of these periods of solitude, when Muhammed was about 40, the angel Gabriel (according to Muslim belief) appeared to him and declared him the Messenger of God. Over the next 22 years Muhammed received messages from time to time, memorized them, and passed them on to his ever-increasing band of followers.

As the number of Muslims (Arabic for "submitted ones") grew, they became unpopular in Mecca, so in 622 Muhammed and several of his disciples fled to the nearby town of Medina. This flight, called the hegira (pronounced HEEJ-rah), marks the beginning of the Arabic calendar (which varies slightly in year-length from the Christian calendar); 2000 A.D. was 1420–1421 A.H. (Anno Hegira). By the end of his life Muhammed had consolidated several Arabian tribes into a powerful military and political force.

The Koran (in Arabic, Qur'an) is a short book—about the length the New Testament would be if Revelation were left off. Conservative Muslims do not believe in translating the Koran into other languages, as they consider it given in the exact words God intended; people wanting to know its message, they believe, should learn Arabic.

Like the New Testament, the Koran is divided into chapters (114 of them, called suras) and verses. After the opening sura, which you have here, the rest are arranged basically by length; this means that reading the Koran straight through can be, for the first-time reader, a rather confusing experience. Extended parts of the Koran overlap with events in the Gospels and, especially, the Old Testament.

SURA (CHAPTER) 1

Praise be to God, the Lord of all creatures: the most merciful, the king of the day of judgment. We worship you and beg assistance of you. Direct us in the right way, the way of those to whom you have been gracious—not the way of those against whom you are angry, nor of those who go astray.

SURA 2 (excerpts)

It is not righteousness to pray to the east or west, but righteousness is believing in God and the Last Day and the angels and the scriptures and the prophets; it is giving money for God's sake to orphans and the needy and strangers and beggars; it is ransoming captives; it is praying. Righteousness is keeping your word and handling hardship and misfortune with patience. These are the signs of the ones who are true, the ones who belong to God.

Fight for the religion of God against those who fight you; but don't sin by attacking them first, because God doesn't like sinners. Kill unbelievers* wherever you find them, because temptation to idolatry is worse than slaughter. But do not fight them in a holy place—unless they attack you, in which case you can kill them. This is what infidels deserve. But if they stop being unbelievers, leave them alone; God is gracious and merciful.

* unbelievers: Muslims differ on this point, but most do not consider Jews and Christians "unbelievers"; that term is usually reserved for atheists, idol-worshipers, etc.

SURA 19 (excerpts)

(NOTE: This is the Koran's version of the Christmas story, the birth of Jesus.)

Remember from this book the story of Mary. When she left her family and went eastward, she took a veil to conceal herself. Then the angel Gabriel appeared to her in the shape of a perfect man. She said, "I am running to God, and he will defend me; if you fear him, you won't approach me."

Gabriel answered, "I am God's messenger and have been sent to give you a son."

Mary said, "How can I have a son, since a man has not touched me? I am a virgin."

The angel replied, "It is going to happen. God has said, 'It is easy for me; I will perform it. He will be a sign to men and a mercy from me, for I have decreed it so.'"

So Mary conceived, and she retired with the baby in her womb to a distant place. The pains of childbirth came upon her near the trunk of a palm tree. She said, "Oh, I wish I had died rather than going through this!"

But a voice from below called to her, saying, "Do not be grieved. God has provided a stream for you. And if you shake the trunk of the palm tree, it shall let down ripe dates upon you, ready to be gathered. So eat, drink, and calm down."

And so Mary returned to her people, carrying a baby in her arms. They said to her, "Mary, this is strange. Your father wasn't a woman-chaser, and your mother didn't run around either."

But Mary decided to let the baby defend her and simply pointed to it. The people said, "What? How can we speak to a baby still in the cradle?"

The baby spoke up and said, "I am God's servant; he has given me the message of the gospel and appointed me as a prophet. He will bless me wherever I go. He has commanded me to pray and to give to the poor as long as I live. God has made me happy and humble, and he causes me to care about my mother. He gave me peace the day I was born, and will give me peace the day I die, and will give me peace the day I come back to life again."

This was Jesus the son of Mary. This is the whole truth, though some people still doubt it. It would be inappropriate for God himself to have a son—God forbid! When he wants something to happen, he simply says "Be!", and it is.

Some people say, "The Almighty has himself begotten a son." This is blasphemy; it's almost enough to make the heavens split and the earth crack in two and the mountains fall down. They actually say God has produced a son. That would not be seemly.

I, God, have given you the Koran in your own language, so that you can easily inform the righteous and warn the wicked.

THE HEPTAMERON

◆

By Marguerite of Navarre (1492–1549)

(Translated by George Saintsbury, contemporized and abridged
by Dr. Marv Hinten)

INTRODUCTION TO MARGUERITE
OF NAVARRE

Marguerite was born in a famous year—to Americans, anyway. She was
also born into royal lineage; in fact, her brother eventually became king
of France. Her status advantage overruled her gender disadvantage, so
Marguerite received a first-class education, by private tutoring, which
she thoroughly took advantage of. Besides her native language of
French, she also learned Greek, Hebrew, Latin, Spanish, German, and
Italian. Her brother became king in 1515, and Marguerite quickly
became one of the leading ladies of the court.

Her first husband having died in 1525, Marguerite remarried shortly
thereafter and became queen of Navarre, a territory on the northern
border of France and Spain. Her daughter, Jeanne, became the mother
of Henry IV, one of the more famous kings of France.

Marguerite's most famous work, *The Heptameron* (from Greek
"hepta," meaning seven) is clearly indebted to a similar work by the

Italian writer Boccaccio. His *Decameron* tells of ten young people who go to an isolated area to escape the plague. To keep from getting bored, they agree that for ten straight days ("deca" being Greek for ten), they will each tell a love story to the others. In Marguerite's version, the ten young people are trapped by a flood, so they also agree to tell stories of love and marriage for ten days. Marguerite died, however, after only 70 stories, or seven days' worth, hence the title

Despite the obvious likenesses between *The Heptameron* and *Decameron*, Marguerite's work differs in some significant ways from the earlier book. First, she has the group equally divided between men and women (Boccaccio used seven men), providing a more balanced perspective. Second, after each story is told, Marguerite has the group discuss in detail whether the story characters behaved appropriately and how closely the story connects with real life. Finally, Marguerite's stories are, in general, somewhat less sexual and more relational than Boccaccio's, although the two works do overlap in this regard.

THE HEPTAMERON

NOTE: The commentary on each story is separated from it by underlining. In the commentary, for the sake of clarity, I have italicized names of female speakers so you can readily distinguish the gender of each speaker.

STORY THIRTY-SIX

The President of Grenoble and his beautiful wife lived in tranquility together. But the husband was much older than the wife, so eventually she fell in love with a young clerk named Nicholas. When the President went to the office in the morning, Nicholas used to enter the bedroom and take his place. This was noticed by a servant of the President's who had served in the household for thirty years, and being faithful he could not help mentioning this to his master.

The President, being a prudent man, said he did not want to believe the story lightly. He said to the servant, "If this is the truth, you can easily prove it; if you can't give proof, I'll have to believe this is a falsehood to create strife between my wife and me." The servant promised he would provide evidence.

So one morning, after the President had gone to the office and Nicholas had entered the bedroom, this servant sent another household employee to tell the master to come; he remained watching at the door to make sure Nicholas didn't leave. When the President received the request to leave, he pretended to be sick, left the office, and went home. He found his old servant at the door and was assured that Nicholas was still inside.

"Don't leave this door," the President said, "because, as you are aware, there is no other way of going into or out of this bedroom, except for the little closet at the back, and I am the only one who has the key to that."

The President entered the room and found his wife and Nicholas in bed together. The clerk threw himself at the President's feet to beg forgiveness, while the wife began to cry. The President responded to his wife, "You have done a terrible deed, but I am unwilling for my home to be dishonored on your account, and I do not want our daughters to be ashamed. Therefore I command you to stop crying and listen to what I am going to do. And you, Nicholas, hide yourself in that closet and do not make a single sound."

When Nicholas was hidden and the wife had stopped crying, the President opened the door and said to the servant outside, "Didn't you assure me that you would show me a man in bed with my wife? Trusting your word, I came home ready to kill her, but I don't see a man in here. And I've searched the whole room!"

Then he made the servant look under both beds and in every part of the room. The servant couldn't find anything and said to his master, "The devil must have done away with him, because I saw a man go in here, and he never did come out this door. But I can't see him in here anywhere."

The President said, "What a wicked servant you are to try to create a fight between my wife and me! So now I have to fire you. However, I'll pay you what I currently owe you, and some more besides. But you have to leave right away; I don't want you still in this town twenty-four hours from now." The servant cried, but the President gave him an extra six years' pay, besides what was owed, and indicated that more money would be coming the servant's way in the future.

After the servant left, the President made Nicholas come out of the closet, and after telling both the clerk and the wife what he thought of their wickedness, he told them not to mention the matter to anyone. He also told his wife to buy herself some new clothes and to start going to more banquets and dances. To Nicholas the President said, "Enjoy yourself and have a good time, but if I ever whisper "Be gone!" in your ear, I want you out of town within three hours." The President then returned to court, and no one else knew what had happened. For the next few weeks, more often than usual, he went to banquets and dances with his wife.

One night at a dance, when his wife was sitting, the President asked Nicholas to dance with her. The clerk, thinking the past had been forgiven and forgotten, gladly did so. But as soon as the dance was over the President whispered in his ear, "Be gone, and never return." Nicholas was grieved to leave his lover, but he was glad to escape with his life.

Things continued this way for months, and all the friends and neighbors and relatives were convinced of the great love the President had for his wife. Then one day in May he went into his garden and gathered some herbs for a salad for his wife. She didn't live long after eating that salad—less than twenty-four hours, in fact. Upon her death the President made such a show of mourning that no one suspected him of having anything to do with her death; in this way he saved the honor of his house.

Ennasuite finished her story by saying, "I do not mean by this to praise the President's conscience, but rather to bring out his great patience and prudence. And I ask you ladies not to be angered by the truth, which sometimes speaks against ourselves as much as against the men."

Parlamente commented, "If all those who have fallen in love with their servants had to eat salads like that one, I know some people who would be less fond of their gardens and would pluck up the herbs from out there."

Her husband Hircan knew why she made this remark and angrily replied, "A virtuous woman should never be judgmental of another person's guilt."

"Knowledge is not judgmentalism," *Parlamente* answered. "I'm merely saying that the President desired revenge yet behaved with great prudence and wisdom."

"And with great malevolence," added *Longarine*. "That was a slow and cruel vengeance, and it showed he cared nothing about either God or conscience."

"Why, what would you want him to do," Hircan asked, "to revenge himself for the greatest wrong a woman can do a man?"

"It would have been different if he had killed her in his initial wrath," answered *Longarine*. "Counselors say the first impulses of passion are not under a person's control, so a sin like that can be more easily forgiven."

"Yes," said Geburon, "but then his daughters would have borne the stain of having an adulterous mother."

"He shouldn't have killed her at all," said *Longarine*, "because when his first wrath had gone past, she might have lived with him virtuously after that, and nothing would ever have been said of the matter."

"Do you think," said Saffredent, "that he had actually calmed down just because he concealed his anger? I think he was as wrathful the day he made that salad as he had been the day it happened, because some people stay worked up emotionally until they've let it out."

STORY FIFTY-FIVE

In the town of Saragossa lived a rich merchant. Weakened by illness, he found death drawing near, which meant he could no longer retain all the goods he had gathered over the years—perhaps not altogether honestly. He decided that if he made a little present to God, to be given after his death, that that might make partial atonement for his sins—money to buy a pardon, in effect. So in his will, after settling his household affairs, he came to a fine Spanish horse that he owned. He said that he wanted this horse to be sold and the money given to the poor. And he even brought this matter to the attention of his wife, telling her to sell the horse just as soon as he was dead, distributing the proceeds to the needy.

Shortly thereafter the merchant died and was buried. The widow went to a longtime household servant and said, "It's bad enough I've just lost a husband; I don't want to lose my possessions as well! Now of course I don't want to disobey his will. In fact, I'll do better; I'll do the sort of thing he would have done if he had stayed alive. Because as you are well aware, he wouldn't have put out even a five-dollar-bill for the poor during his lifetime, no matter how great the need was. But promise me to keep our plan a secret."

The servant did, so she continued: "Go sell the horse, and when you are asked how much you want for it, say, 'A dollar.' But then add, 'I also have a cat I want to sell with the horse, and the cat is another $499, making $500 altogether.'"

So the servant went out to the marketplace. He walked the horse all around for people to see, holding the cat in his arms. A gentleman saw the horse, began examining it, and liked what he saw. "How much do you want for this horse?" he asked.

"One dollar," replied the servant.

"No, seriously," responded the gentleman.

"I am serious," said the servant. "This is a one-dollar horse. However, I have here a $499 cat to go with it, and I can't sell the horse without the cat. They're a matched set."

The gentleman thought that was a reasonable price to pay, so they made the transactions consecutively, $1 for the horse, $499 for the cat, and the deal was over.

The servant brought home the money, and the widow was quite pleased. She gave the entire dollar to the poor, the full price of the horse, and the cat money she kept to spend on herself and the family and servants.

"Well, what do you think?" asked *Nomerfide*, the storyteller. "Wasn't she a lot sharper than her husband?"

"I think she did the right thing," *Parlamente* commented. "Her husband's wits were probably wandering there at the end, and since she knew her husband, she knew that he would really want the money to stay in the family. What she did was very wise."

"What!" roared Geburon. "You don't think it's wrong to go against the expressed will of a dying man?"

"Of course it's wrong—unless you think the man has gone out of his mind," answered *Parlamente.*

"Do you call it out of your mind to give money to the poor?"

"No," replied *Parlamente,* "if a man is giving away his own money. But to give away money that belongs to other people is crazy. Sometimes you see merchants who have robbed people of a hundred thousand dollars over the years give ten thousand to a cathedral's building program to please God. They must think God doesn't know how to count."

Oisille observed, "I've often wondered how people think they can make God happy by donating to things he wasn't interested in while he was on earth, such as fancy buildings, religious artwork, and so on. After all, God said in the book of Psalms that the only offering he absolutely requires from us is a humble and repentant heart. As far as adorning temples goes, St. Paul says in 2 Corinthians that we are the temples that God most wants to dwell in. So you would think people would want to offer themselves while they are still alive, and not ask people to give money to save their souls after they die. God won't judge money, but people's love for him."

Geburon noted, "You wouldn't be able to tell this from listening to ministers and priests tell about how important it is to give money to their building programs."

PARADISE LOST

◆

By John Milton (1667)

(Contemporized and abridged by Dr. Marv Hinten)

INTRODUCTION TO JOHN MILTON (1608–1674)

Milton's father, a London banker, provided him an excellent education, including tutors, private schools, and Cambridge University. From his early years Milton was interested in poetry, and he particularly wanted to write an epic poem in the tradition of Homer and Dante.

But after Milton's college graduation, England was a troubled country. Parliament and King Charles I were at odds, and as Parliament (with a strong Puritan influence) became stronger, Milton rose with it, becoming a member of Oliver Cromwell's political councils. When Charles was beheaded in 1649, Milton wrote pamphlets defending the action.

Milton stayed involved in politics during the next decade, despite the loss of his sight, which disappeared gradually during the 1640s and left him totally blind by about 1650. This political involvement caused Milton's imprisonment when the British monarchy was restored in 1660. In a somewhat surprising decision, however, Milton was released fairly quickly, and he turned his attention to writing his epic.

Paradise Lost covers 12,000 lines, divided into twelve sections called books. By far the most famous section is Book 9, from which this excerpt is taken; it retells the Biblical story of Adam and Eve in the Garden of Eden eating the forbidden fruit, the "fall of humanity" and loss of the right to live in paradise (hence the title). This section is an abridgement of lines 532 to 885 from Book 9 of the original.

PARADISE LOST

NOTE: The original was written entirely in iambic pentameter (ten syllables per line), which has not been reproduced here. This excerpt begins with Satan in the body of a serpent speaking to Eve for the first time.

"Wonder not, sovereign mistress, who are a wonder yourself,
That I approach you thus. All living things gaze on you,
And adore your celestial beauty. But here in this enclosure
Who sees you except one man? And what is one? You should be seen
As a goddess amongst gods, adored and served."   5
        Eve in amazement spoke an answer:
"What may this mean? Language of man pronounced
By tongue of brute, and human sense expressed?
How did you learn to speak, and how did you seem
To grow so wise above the other beasts?"   10
        To her the wily tempter thus replied:
"I was at first like other beasts; till one day roving the field,
I chanced to behold a goodly tree far distant,
Loaded with fruit of fairest colors mixed, red and gold.
I nearer drew to gaze.   15
Around the mossy trunk I wound around, for the branches
Are high off the ground and would require your utmost reach.
The other beasts saw the fruit and wanted it, but couldn't reach.
Up in the tree I ate my fill; I've never had more pleasure,
Whether in eating or drinking.   20
Eventually I perceived a strange alteration within myself;
My thoughts became higher, and I could speak.
But of all the things I looked upon and thought about,
There was nothing more beautiful than yourself."

Eve asked, "Where is this tree?"   25
    The serpent said, "Not far away. I'll take you there myself."
He took Eve to the forbidden tree. When she saw which tree
    It was, she said to her guide:
"This is a fruitless trip, though fruit is here in plenty.
This plant is indeed a wonder, if it caused such effects in you,   30
But of this tree I may not taste nor touch;
God so commanded. Otherwise, we may do what we like."
    To her the tempter guilefully replied:
"Indeed? God says you can do whatever you want,
But you can't eat fruit from the trees?"   35
    Eve the sinless answered: "We can eat fruit
From any tree we want, except this one. God said,
'You can't eat from this one; if you do, you'll die.'"
At this the serpent acted passionately indignant.
    "Queen of the Universe, don't believe these death threats!   40
You won't die! How could you die? From the fruit?
It gives life and knowledge. From the Threatener?
Look at me; I ate and live. In fact, I'm higher than I was before!
Can beasts get higher, but not people? Do you really think
God would get mad over such a petty little thing   45
And send you death, whatever that might be?
God said it's a tree of knowledge; isn't that a good thing?
So why was the tree forbidden?
I'll tell you why. It's to keep you and Adam in awe,
To keep you low and ignorant, his worshipers.   50
God knows that the day you eat from this, you'll be like gods,
Knowing both good and evil like he does.
It's a matter of proportion that you would be a god,
Since I became like man. Perhaps that's what death means;
Perhaps it's putting off humanity and becoming a god.   55
That's a death to be wished!"

He ended, and his words filled with slyness
Made easy way into her heart. Fixed on the fruit she gazed.
Meanwhile the hour of noon drew on, and woke
An eager appetite, raised by the smell so savory of that fruit;   60
And so Eve began to think to herself:
    "In the day we eat of this fair fruit, God said, we shall die.
How dies the serpent? He has eaten and lives, and knows,
And speaks, and reasons. He was irrational before.
For us alone was death invented? Or to us alone   65
Is intellectual food denied? It seems for beasts;
Yet the first beast who ate brings us to the tree with joy.
It's a fruit fair to the eye, inviting to the taste, able to make wise;
Why shouldn't I have some now, and feed at once
My body and my mind?"   70
    So saying, her rash hand in evil hour forth reaching to the fruit,
She plucked and ate. Earth felt the wound. Back to the thicket
Slunk the guilty serpent, but it mattered not, for Eve now
Was intent wholly on her taste. She noted nothing else.
It seemed she had never tasted such delight until then, whether it
was true   75
Or simply imagined so, for she had high expectations of knowledge—
Nor was Godhead from her thought. Greedily she engorged
Without restraint, eating death. At last, heightened as if with wine,
Pleased with herself she thus began:
    "O sovereign, virtuous, most precious of all trees in Paradise!   80
Henceforth I will tend to you every day, till daily eating
Makes me mature in knowledge. But what shall I tell Adam?
Shall I make known to him my change, and give him some
To partake full happiness with me? Or should I keep
The odds in my favor, to make me more equal to him.   85
Or perhaps, someday, superior. That's not undesirable.
For inferior, who is free? That's a good idea.

But what if God has seen, and death ensues? Then Adam
Will be wedded to another Eve, with me extinct.
That's a death just to think about. So I'm confirmed;   90
Adam will share with me in bliss or woe."
     So saying, from the tree her step she turned, but first
A low bow made, as to the power that dwelt within.
And so she hastened to Adam, these words to him addressed:
     "Have you not wondered, Adam, where I've been?   95
My reason is a strange one, and wonderful to hear.
That tree is not, as we were told, a danger tree—oh no!
It has divine effect to open eyes, and make those gods who taste.
It has been tasted twice. The serpent wise, either not restrained
As we are, or else not obeying, has eaten of the fruit   100
And has become, not dead, as we were threatened,
But given human voice and human sense. It reasoned with me
So admirably, and spoke so persuasively, that I also have tasted,
And have also found my eyes opener, growing up to godhood,
Which for you chiefly I sought, without you can despise;   105
For bliss is only bliss to me if you have part.
Without you, it would be tedious. So you taste too, so we
Will have an equal share, and join in equal joy, as now
We have equal love—from fear that, you not tasting,
We shall be too different to be together joined.   110

ENGLISH RENAISSANCE POETRY

◆

LET ME NOT (SONNET 116) by William Shakespeare (1564–1616)

Let me not to the marriage of true minds
Admit impediments; love is not love   impediments: obstacles
Which alters when it alteration finds,
Or bends with the remover to remove.
O no, it is an ever-fixed mark
That looks on tempests and is never shaken;
It is the star to every wandering bark   bark: ship
Whose worth and height cannot be ever taken.
Love's not time's fool, though rosy lips and cheeks
Within his bending sickle's blade do come;
Love alters not with his brief hours and weeks
But bears it out even to the edge of doom.
    If this be error, and upon me proved,
    I never wrote, nor no one ever loved.

SONG TO CELIA by Ben Jonson (1572–1637)

Drink to me only with thine eyes
  And I will pledge with mine;
Or leave a kiss but in the cup
  And I'll not look for wine.
The thirst that from the soul does rise
  Does ask a drink divine;
But might I of Jove's nectar sup,   Jove: king of the gods
  I would not change for thine.

I sent thee late a rosy wreath   late: lately
  Not so much honoring thee
As giving it a hope that there   *felt sorry for the roses*
  It could not withered be.
But thou thereon didst only breathe
  And sent it back to me;
Since then it grows and smells, I swear,
  Not of itself, but thee.

THE PASSIONATE SHEPHERD TO HIS LOVE
by Christopher Marlowe (1564–1593) (abridged)

Come live with me and be my love,
And we will all the pleasures prove
That valleys, hillsides, groves, and fields,
Woods, or steepy mountain yields.

And I will make you beds of roses   5
And a thousand fragrant posies,
A cap of flowers, and a kirtle   kirtle: skirt
Embroidered all with leaves of myrtle.   myrtle: a type of tree

And shepherd friends will dance and sing
For your delight each May morning;   10
If these delights your mind may move,
Then live with me and be my love.

THE NYMPH'S REPLY TO THE SHEPHERD by Walter Raleigh
(1552–1618) (abridged)

If all the world and love were young
And truth in every shepherd's tongue,
These pretty pleasures might me move
To live with you and be your love.

Your many gifts, your beds of roses,   5
Your caps, your kirtles, and your posies,
Soon break, soon wither, are forgotten—
In passion ripe, in reason rotten.

But could youth last and love still breed,   9
Had joys no date nor age no need,   date: expiration date
Then these delights my mind might move
To live with you and be your love.

ON A GIRDLE by Edmund Waller (1606–1687)

That which her slender waist confined,
Shall now my joyful temples bind;
No monarch but would give his crown,
His arms might do what this has done.

It was my heaven's extremest sphere,   5
The fence that held my lovely deer;
My joy, my grief, my hope, my love
Did all within this circle move.

A narrow compass, and yet there
Dwelt all that's good and all that's fair;   10
Give me but what this ribbon bound,
Take all the rest the sun goes round!

PARADISE by George Herbert

NOTE: In some places I have kept the old-fashioned spelling.

I bless you, Lord, because I GROW
Among your trees, which in a ROW
To you both fruit and order OW.

What open force, or hidden CHARM
Can blast my fruit, or bring me HARM   5
While the enclosure is your ARM?

Enclose me still for fear I START.   start: become startled
and run away

Be to me rather sharp and TART
Than let me lack your hand and ART.

When you do greater judgments SPARE   10
And with your knife just prune and PARE
Even fruitful trees more fruitful ARE.

Such sharpness shows the sweetest FREND;
Such cuttings rather heal than REND   rend: tear apart
And such beginnings touch their END.   touch their end: achieve
                                              their goal

SUBMISSION by George Herbert (1593–1633)

NOTE: Upon graduating with honors from Cambridge University, Herbert expected to receive a major government position. He did not and was greatly disappointed. This poem is his attempt to come to terms with that disappointment.

Although you are my wisdom, Lord,
And both my eyes are thine,
My mind becomes extremely stirred
From missing my design.

Were it not better to bestow   5
Some place and power on me?
Then should thy praises with me grow
And share in my degree.

But when I thus dispute and grieve
I do resume my sight,   10
And stealing what I once did give
I take from you your right.

How know I, if you should me raise,
That I should then raise thee?
Perhaps great places and your praise   15
Do not so well agree.

Therefore unto my place I stand;
I will no more advise:
Only do thou lend me a hand,
Since you have both my eyes.   20

UPON JULIA'S VOICE by Robert Herrick (1591–1674)

So smooth, so sweet, so silvery is your voice,
That, could they hear it, the damned would make no noise,
But listen to you, walking in your chamber,
Melting melodious words to lutes of amber.   lute: an early guitar

LaVergne, TN USA
27 July 2010
191122LV00004B/4/A